About the Author

Len Driscoll is the pen name for author Frank Dirscherl, best known for his many novels in *The Wraith Dread Avenger of the Underworld* series, including the Amazon bestselling *The Wraith* and *Sanderson of Metro,* as well as several short stories. *The Black Seam* is the second in the *George 'Magpie' Collins mystery* series.

A librarian with over thirty years experience, Frank has also worked at a book wholesaler, a specialist medical practice and as a tutor in the writing and producing of comic books. His interests include reading, traveling, politics, architecture and the environment.

Frank lives in the Illawarra on the south coast of New South Wales, Australia, with his wife and daughter, and is always working on his latest literary endeavours.

GLOWING EYES MEDIA

Praise for *Sanderson of Metro*
Amazon bestseller

"Once shrouded in mystery, The Wraith's stunning origin is finally revealed. Dirscherl and Nash have written one hell of an adventure novel filled with myth, intrigue, and excitement. Highly recommended reading."
- A.P. Fuchs, writer, *The Axiom-man Saga, The Way of the Fog, Undead World trilogy*

"Recommended for Wraith and pulp hero fans."
– Leon Mallett, *Amazon*

"At the end of the day, this novel is a worthy addition to The Wraith's continuing story and a necessary purchase if you're a fan of the character. It's also just a flat out enjoyable reading experience."
– Marcus Bucklin, *Amazon*

"The story is well written, and the Paul Sanderson character fleshed out fairly well...I highly recommend this well written entry for all comic book fans."
– Virginia E. Johnson, *Amazon*

Praise for *The Wraith*
Amazon bestseller

"I love the coloring job and specially the 'glowing' eyes on the chest of the character."
- Guillermo del Toro, director, *Blade II, Hellboy I & II*

"I liked the story a lot... It's a very strong debut."
Steve Englehart, writer, *Detective Comics, The Avengers, Green Lantern*

"I have read the novel (I couldn't put it down)... It is amazing to see how her (Leena) character evolves from Part I to Part II. At first she appears as every other 'girlfriend' in an action film, but those twelve months that pass obviously change her as a person and I love the person she becomes: tougher, but still human."
- Amber Moelter, actress, *Catwoman: Copycat*

"I finished *The Wraith* book last night. I must say I enjoyed it quite a bit. The scenes kept playing in my head like a big budget Hollywood film. I mentioned earlier that I enjoy when the hero is put to the test physically and doesn't win the battle unscathed. Boy, (Frank) delivered that in spades!"
- Jeff Welborn, artist, *Nightmare World, The Wraith*

"Genius + sweat + dedication = hard hittin' hero action! Go Aussie!"
- Dan Lennard, writer, *People* magazine

"*The Wraith* is a wonderful throwback to the purple prose of the bloody pulps with a hero clearly descendant from the likes of the Shadow and the Spider. A fast, action-packed thrill-ride with great characters, both noble and villainous. Slam-bang kick off to a super new series. One I'm anxious to follow."

   – Ron Fortier, writer, *The Spider, Brother Bones, Domino Lady*

"I became familiar with Frank Dirscherl's The Wraith from the comic book of the same name. When the first Wraith novel came out I just had to read it. I was not disappointed. The Wraith is a fast-paced thrill-ride. I'm looking forward to the upcoming sequel."

   – Bobby Nash, writer, *Evil Ways, Fantastix, Lance Star*

"*The Wraith* (is) a really fun read. Have been a fan of Kenneth Robeson's Doc Savage and The Avenger books for years... *The Wraith* reminds me of Robeson at his best."

   – G.R. Lawson, Publisher, General Jinjur Comics

"A short, pulp, superhero novel... Clearly more adventures to come with how this is set up."

   – Richard Scott, *Super Reader* website

"*The Wraith* is an enlightening journey into the darkness of superhero fiction, and a worthy entry into both pulpdom and comicdom."

   – Kevin Noel Olson, *Silver Bullet Comics* website

"*The Wraith* is a testament to Frank's dedication and talent. Other small press characters have come and gone, but The Wraith endures, because Frank understands what makes a classic character."

    – Richard Evans, writer, *The Canadian Legion*

"When it comes to superhero fiction and classic pulp stories, Frank Dirscherl channels those classic adventures of the past into *The Wraith* with ease and gives you a hero to believe in."

    – Stephen J. Semones, writer/director, *Beyond the Lens, Crossfire, The Wraith: Eyes of Judgment*

"Frank Dirscherl's writing is action-packed and reminds me why superhero fiction is so much fun in the first place!"

    – A.P. Fuchs, writer, *The Axiom-man Saga, The Way of the Fog, Undead World trilogy*

"Totally enjoyed this book. Good story, a real hero vs villain yarn. Can't wait to read the other adventures of The Wraith."

    – J. Newey, *Amazon*

Praise for *Valley of Evil*

"The second Wraith novel is an improvement, I think. Right from the start Dirscherl throws you into the middle of crazy action.... This book is a whole lot of superheroic pulp fun, and the good news is there seems to be more to come...I look forward to some more of the same."

— Richard Scott, *Super Reader* website

"I think (Dirscherl) really captured a noir element with (his) voice."

— Joshua Gamon, writer, *Abigail & Rox, Digital Webbing Presents*

"I did quite enjoy the books. Best of all, it wasn't overly sex-filled or gory—I can't stand most modern superhero comics that show such things or have the heroes just swear and swear. So *The Wraith* (and *Valley of Evil*) was just up my alley."

— Greg Gick, writer, *The Werewolf of Rutherford Grange, Tales of the Shadowmen, Secret Agent X Vol. 2*

"The Dread Avenger is back. After battling the Cobra in his first prose adventure, The Wraith returns to face all new challenges from Metro City's greatest villains, most notably Hong Kong drug kingpin Ma Tzi. As with his first Wraith novel, Frank Dirscherl treats us to a pulp-inspired adventure that keeps readers on the edge of their seat. You have to read this novel in one sitting."

— Bobby Nash, writer, *Evil Ways, Fantastix, Lance Star*

"In the past five years there has been a tremendous resurgence in pulp fiction centering on the old heroic pulps. Young writers have started taking up the mantle of old masters like Walter Gibson and Lester Dent and begun creating their own avengers in tales of genuine purple prose. Among the best of this new generation of wordsmiths is Australian, Frank Dirscherl and the exploits of his modern pulp paladin, The Wraith. This is grand pulp!"

   – Ron Fortier, writer, *The Spider, Brother Bones, Domino Lady*

Praise for *Crossfire*

"Stephen did a fantastic job of bringing Frank Dirscherl's character to life!"

    – Adam DiTroia, composer, *The Wraith: Eyes of Judgment*, MTV, Fox Sports

"Loved the book!! Can't wait for the next installment..."

    – Larry Mainland, actor, *The Walking Dead, Lawless, The Three Stooges*

"The action comes swift, and doesn't stop until the final pages. *Crossfire* tells a great story of betrayal and revenge."

    – C.R. Blevins, writer, *A Western Tale*

"This was my first introduction to The Wraith and I was not disappointed. The action comes swift, and doesn't stop until the final pages.... If you love a good action/hero story, you will certainly enjoy reading *Crossfire.*"

    – Ally, *Amazon*

"Makes me want more...should be the next series on Netflix..."

    – Bill Lancaster, *Amazon*

"Another excellent entry in The Wraith Adventures series. Thoroughly recommended for Wraith fans and fans of pulp super-heroics."

    – Leon Mallett, *Amazon*

Praise for *Cult of the Damned*

"Only by the first three pages, Frank Dirscherl wonderfully captures a dark and mysterious atmosphere, one that leaves the reader with a cryptic and eerie sensation; one that makes me cold just thinking about it."

>   – Rennie Cowan, writer/director, *The Thriller Idol: A Tribute to the Legacy of Michael Jackson, Kade the Conqueror*

"Frank Dirscherl pulls you into the world of The Wraith from the first sentence and refuses to let you go until the last one."

>   – Stephen J. Semones, writer/director, *Beyond the Lens, Crossfire, The Wraith: Eyes of Judgment*

"The Wraith is one of my favorite characters and every time Frank Dirscherl puts pen to paper I know I'm in for a real treat."

>   – A.P. Fuchs, writer, *The Axiom-man Saga, The Way of the Fog, Undead World trilogy*

Praise for *Cry of the Werewolf*

"Frank Dirscherl delivers beyond measure.... The solid characters, settings and story really propel you page to page and leave you hanging on for more."
- Stephen J. Semones, writer/director, *Beyond the Lens, Crossfire, The Wraith: Eyes of Judgment*

"Each new installment in *The Wraith Adventures* series is a guaranteed good time filled with high adventure, romance and pulpy fun. Dirscherl is at the top of his form."
- A.P. Fuchs, writer, *The Axiom-man Saga, The Way of the Fog, Undead World trilogy*

"The writing is well done and well edited, and is filled with that distinct Dirscherl style of pulp that I enjoy so much. The book is a perfect example of what Neo Pulp/Superhero and Horror fiction can be and is a worthy addition to any fan's collection."
- Marcus Bucklin, *Amazon*

Praise for *Vendetta*

"...in all a great brew that had me hooked for the whole ride. Now bring on the next book, Frank..."

– Leon Mallett, *Amazon*

"This book starts with a literal bang and doesn't let the foot off of the gas until the very last page. The book is well plotted and moves at a breakneck pace, making it an enjoyable, short read. I loved this book very much as a fan of The Wraith and I believe that anyone who is a fan of the series should consider this required reading."

– Marcus Bucklin, *Amazon*

Praise for *Zombies Attack!* in *Metahumans vs the Undead*

"This compilation of superheroes vs evil offers top entertainment for superhero lovers! Frank Dirscherl and others are at their best with their contributed stories. I will now pursue other stories written by these authors, such as those involving Mr Dirscherl's The Wraith. This type of reading enjoyment knows no end!"

– Ramona Wingart, writer, *Where is Brother Beaver?*, *Emily Suzanne Smith!*

Praise for *Werewolves Attack!* in *Metahumans vs Werewolves*

"Always a great read. Can never put it down once you get started... "

– Geraldine L. Lewis, *Amazon*

BY LEN DRISCOLL

FICTION

the *George 'Magpie' Collins mystery* series

1. *The Broken Chain*
2. *The Black Seam*
3. *The Magpie's Shadow* - COMING SOON

BY FRANK DIRSCHERL

The Wraith Dread Avenger of the Underworld series

1. *The Wraith*
2. *Valley of Evil*
3. *Crossfire* (with Stephen J. Semones)
4. *Cult of the Damned*
5. *Cry of the Werewolf*
6. *Swamp Witch of Satan's Forest* (with Ray MacKay)
7. *Vendetta*
8. *Lady Wraith* (with Adam Oravec)
9. *Kingdom*
10. *City of Fear*
11. *Birds of the Living Dead* - COMING SOON

12. *The Acolyte* - COMING SOON

Books of Judgment

1. *Sanderson of Metro* (with Bobby Nash)
2. *Serpent Rising* (with Greg Gick)
3. *Rising Son* (with Adam Oravec) - COMING SOON

SHORT STORY COLLECTIONS

The Wraith Vol. 1
The Wraith Vol. 2 - COMING SOON
Lance Star – Sky Ranger Vol. 1

NON-FICTION

The Hitchers of Oz
Beyond the Lens (edited)

THE BLACK SEAM

a George 'Magpie' Collins mystery #2

by

Len Driscoll

GLOWING EYES MEDIA
WOLLONGONG

GLOWING EYES MEDIA
PO Box 31
Wollongong NSW 2520

ISBN 978-0-646-72816-2

THE BLACK SEAM

PUBLISHED BY GLOWING EYES MEDIA, October 2025
www.glowingeyesmedia.com
FRONT COVER ART by Chaz Gupta
COVER LAYOUT AND DESIGN AND INTERIOR DESIGN by Frank Dirscherl
EDITED by Claude Aylmer
FIRST EDITION

For more on *The Black Seam*
visit www.glowingeyesmedia.com

Text set in Garamond-Normal. Printed and bound in the USA

A catalogue record for this book is available from the National Library of Australia

To Ross MacDonald...my literary inspiration

THE BLACK SEAM

~ Chapter 1 ~

The morning rain had left Castlereagh Street looking like a dark mirror, reflecting the grey April sky back at itself. I was nursing my second cup of black coffee and trying to make sense of the morning paper's headlines when she walked into my office. She didn't knock—just opened the door like she owned the place and stood there dripping rain onto my hardwood floor.

Dr Eleanor Whitman, as I was soon to discover, was the sort of woman who'd learned to carry herself like she had answers to questions other people hadn't thought to ask yet. Tall, with steel-grey hair pulled back in a way that suggested she didn't have time for nonsense, she wore a dark wool coat that probably cost more than most blokes made in a month. But there was something in her eyes that didn't match the confident posture—a kind of hunted look that I'd seen before in people who'd found themselves in deeper water than they'd bargained for.

"Mr Collins?" Her voice had the educated tones of someone who'd spent years telling other people what was wrong with them. "I need your help."

I gestured to the chair across from my desk. "That's what the sign on the door says. Though most people make an appointment first."

She sat down carefully, keeping her handbag clutched tight in her lap. "I couldn't risk using the telephone. This is...delicate."

I'd heard that word before. In my experience, when respectable people said something was delicate, it usually meant someone was about to get hurt. I leaned back in my chair and waited for her to tell me about it.

"My name is Dr Eleanor Whitman. I run a private psychiatric clinic in Woollahra," she began, then stopped as if the words had got stuck somewhere between her brain and her mouth. "I specialise in treating patients with...difficult conditions. Depression, anxiety, trauma from the war."

"Worthwhile work," I said, though I kept my voice neutral. In my line of business, you learned not to judge people by their professions—sometimes the most respectable jobs hid the darkest secrets.

She opened her handbag and pulled out an envelope. The paper was expensive, cream-coloured, the sort that told you whoever wrote it had money to burn. "Three days ago, I received this."

I took the envelope and slid out a single sheet of paper. The message was typed, probably on a Remington by the look of the letters, and whoever had written it knew how to get to the point:

Dr Whitman,

You have broken the seam of trust that should exist between doctor and patient. The methods you have used go beyond unorthodox—they are criminal. I have evidence of your violations of medical ethics and patient confidentiality that would destroy your career and see you struck off the medical register.

If you wish to avoid public exposure, you will place £500 in unmarked notes in a suitcase and leave it at the luggage counter at Central Station on Friday at 3 PM. Further instructions will follow.

Remember, doctor—broken seams will be exposed.

I read it through twice, then looked up at her. "Any idea who might have written this?"

"None." Her voice was steady, but I could see the tension in the way she held her shoulders. "I've been over my patient files, my staff, everyone who might have access to confidential information. I simply don't know."

"The note mentions breaking the seam of trust. Methods that go beyond unorthodox. Care to elaborate on what that might mean?"

She was quiet for a long moment, staring at her hands. When she looked up, there was something vulnerable in her expression that hadn't been there before. "I use some...experimental techniques in my practice. Hypnosis, combined with certain pharmaceutical aids. Nothing harmful, but perhaps not entirely conventional."

"Pharmaceutical aids?"

"Mild sedatives. Sodium pentothal in very small doses. It helps patients access suppressed memories, traumatic experiences they've buried." She leaned forward slightly. "Mr Collins, I want you to understand—I would never deliberately harm a patient. Everything I do is in service of helping them heal."

I nodded and set the letter down on my desk. "Tell me about your patients. Anyone leave recently under difficult circumstances?"

"Several, actually." She hesitated. "It's not uncommon in psychiatric treatment. Patients often resist therapy when it becomes...challenging."

"Anyone in particular stand out?"

"There was a young man. Robert Ashford. He was the son of Charles Ashford, the mining magnate. Robert had been through a traumatic experience—an accident at one of his father's mines where several workers were killed. He felt responsible, developed severe depression and anxiety."

"When did he leave your care?"

"Two months ago. He...he took his own life shortly after."

I felt that familiar tightness in my chest that came when a case started to show its teeth. "Suicide?"

"The coroner ruled it accidental death. Robert had been drinking, fell from a cliff in the Blue Mountains where he was staying." She looked down at her hands again. "But I knew Robert. He was getting better, or so I thought. The suicide...it shocked me."

"And you think there might be a connection between his death and this blackmail?"

"I don't know. Maybe. Robert had been making remarkable progress, and then suddenly he left treatment and was dead within a fortnight." She met my eyes. "Mr Collins, I need you to find out who's doing this to me. I can't pay that money—I don't have it, for one thing. But more importantly, I won't be extorted by someone who doesn't understand the complexities of psychiatric treatment."

I studied her face, trying to read the truth behind the professional mask. In my experience, people who claimed they were being blackmailed usually had something worth blackmailing them about. But there was something in her manner that suggested she was more frightened than guilty.

"My fee is five pounds a day plus expenses," I said finally. "And I'll need complete access to your clinic, your staff, and your records."

"Of course." She reached into her handbag and pulled out a roll of notes. "Here's twenty pounds as a retainer. Will that be sufficient?"

I took the money and locked it in my desk drawer. "Tell me about your staff. Anyone who might have access to confidential patient information?"

"There's Patricia Mills, my nurse. She's been with me for eight months. And James Hartwell, who handles the administrative side—appointments, billing, that sort of thing. He's been with me for two years."

"Anyone else?"

"A cleaning woman who comes in twice a week. Mrs Davies. She's been with me since I opened the clinic three years ago."

I made notes as she talked, already forming a mental picture of the people I'd need to interview. "One more question, Doctor. This experimental treatment you mentioned—hypnosis and pharmaceutical aids. Ever have any patients react badly to it?"

She was quiet for a long moment. "Psychiatric treatment is always risky, Mr Collins. The human mind is fragile, and sometimes trying to heal it can cause... complications."

"What kind of complications?"

"Memory issues. Confusion. In rare cases, patients might develop false memories or become unable to distinguish between real and imagined experiences." She stood up, smoothing down her coat. "But I want to emphasise—I would never deliberately harm a patient. Everything I do is guided by my oath to do no harm."

I walked her to the door, noting how she moved with the careful precision of someone who'd learned to control every gesture. "I'll start with your clinic tomorrow morning. In the meantime, don't do anything about this demand. If whoever wrote this is watching, we want them to think you're going to cooperate."

She nodded and shook my hand. Her grip was firm, but I could feel the slight tremor in her fingers. "Thank you, Mr Collins. I hope you can resolve this quickly."

After she left, I sat back down at my desk and read the blackmail note again. The phrase 'broken seams will be exposed' stuck in my mind. It had the ring of someone who thought they were being clever, but it might also be a clue. In my experience, blackmailers usually couldn't resist showing off how much they knew.

I pulled out a fresh notebook and wrote "Dr Eleanor Whitman" at the top of the first page. Underneath, I made a list: Patricia Mills, James Hartwell, Mrs Davies, Robert Ashford (deceased). Then I added a question mark and the word 'others.'

The rain had stopped, and pale sunlight was filtering through the grimy windows of my office. I could hear the traffic on Castlereagh Street picking up as the lunch crowd began to move. My stomach reminded me that I'd skipped breakfast, but I wanted to think through what I'd learned before I headed over to the Masonic Club for a meal.

Dr Whitman's story had the feel of truth to it, but there were gaps—things she hadn't told me or didn't want to tell me. The experimental treatments, the connection to Robert Ashford's death, the specific phrasing of the blackmail note. Someone knew enough about her practice to cause real damage, and they were professional enough to typewrite their demands rather than hand-write them.

I locked the blackmail note in my desk drawer next to the retainer money and grabbed my coat. The case felt like it had depths I hadn't seen yet, but that was nothing new. In my line of work, the surface was usually the least interesting part of any story.

As I walked over to the club next door, I found myself thinking about seams and broken links. Seams, like chains, were only as strong as their weakest point. The trick was finding that weakness and applying just enough pressure to make the whole thing fall apart.

Someone was applying pressure to Dr Eleanor Whitman. The question was whether they were trying to break her, or whether she was just one link in something much larger.

~ Chapter 2 ~

The next morning brought one of those crisp April days that made Sydney feel like it was trying to apologize for the rain. I caught the tram to Woollahra, watching the city change from the grimy commercial bustle of the CBD to the leafy respectability of the eastern suburbs. Dr Whitman's clinic occupied a converted Victorian mansion on a quiet street lined with jacarandas, the sort of place where people paid good money to have their problems solved discreetly.

The brass nameplate beside the front door read "Whitman Psychiatric Clinic - Private Consultations by Appointment." I pressed the bell and waited, studying the building's façade. It had been designed to look reassuring rather than clinical—warm sandstone, well-maintained gardens, lace curtains in the windows. The sort of place where wealthy families could send their troubled relatives without admitting they were doing anything so vulgar as seeking psychiatric treatment.

The door opened to reveal a young woman in a starched white uniform. She was pretty in a careful way, with dark hair pinned back and intelligent brown eyes that seemed to take in everything at once. But there was something in her expression that reminded me of a cat watching a mousehole—alert, patient, waiting for something to happen.

"Mr Collins? I'm Patricia Mills, the nurse working for Dr Whitman. She told me you'd be coming by this morning."

I followed her through a reception area that could have belonged to any well-appointed professional office. Dark wood paneling, leather furniture, medical journals arranged on side tables. The only hint of the building's true purpose was a faint medicinal smell that no amount of furniture polish could quite mask.

"Dr Whitman is with a patient at the moment," Patricia said, leading me down a hallway lined with closed doors. "She asked me to show you around first, familiarize you with how we operate."

She opened a door to reveal what had once been a dining room but now served as a treatment room. A leather chair dominated the center, angled to face a smaller seat where the doctor would sit. Medical equipment lined the walls—strange devices with dials and switches that looked like they belonged in a laboratory rather than a consulting room.

"This is where Dr Whitman conducts her individual sessions," Patricia explained, but her voice had taken on a careful quality, as if she was reciting lines she'd memorized. "She specializes in helping patients access suppressed memories, particularly those related to traumatic experiences."

I walked around the chair, noting the leather restraints attached to the arms. "Restraints seem a bit unusual for a psychiatric consultation."

"Some patients become agitated when confronting difficult memories," she said quickly. "It's for their own safety, really. Dr Whitman would never use them inappropriately."

The way she said it made me think she was trying to convince herself as much as me. I made a mental note to ask more about the restraints later, when Patricia wasn't around to provide the official explanation.

"Tell me about the other staff," I said, pulling out my notebook. "Dr Whitman mentioned a secretary?"

"James Hartwell. He handles appointments, billing, patient records. He's been with the clinic for two years." She paused, then added, "He's very dedicated to his work."

"And you've been here eight months?"

"Yes. I came from Royal Prince Alfred Hospital. I was looking for something more... specialized." She smoothed down her uniform in a gesture that seemed unconscious. "Dr Whitman's methods are quite advanced. Not everyone understands what she's trying to accomplish."

I jotted down notes as she talked, but I was watching her face more than listening to her words. There was something she wasn't telling me, something that made her choose her words too carefully and avoid my eyes when she spoke about the doctor's methods.

"Any patients stand out as particularly difficult?" I asked. "Anyone leave under unusual circumstances?"

For just a moment, her composure cracked. Her hand went to her throat, and she looked toward the door as if checking to make sure we weren't being overheard.

"There have been some...challenging cases," she said finally. "Patients who didn't respond well to treatment. But that's not unusual in psychiatric work. Some people aren't ready to face their problems."

"Dr Whitman mentioned Robert Ashford. What can you tell me about him?"

The question hit her like a physical blow. She took a half-step backward, her face going pale beneath the careful makeup.

"Robert was...he was a troubled young man," she said, her voice barely above a whisper. "He'd been through a terrible experience. Dr Whitman worked very hard to help him, but sometimes..." She trailed off, then seemed to gather herself. "Sometimes the mind protects itself by forgetting. When you try to force those memories back, it can be dangerous."

"Dangerous how?"

"Confusion. Disorientation. Sometimes patients can't tell the difference between what really happened and what they think happened." She was speaking faster now, as if she wanted to get the words out before she lost her nerve. "Robert became convinced that he was responsible for things that weren't his fault. Dr Whitman tried to help him see the truth, but he couldn't accept it."

I was about to ask more when footsteps echoed in the hallway outside. Patricia's head snapped up, and the professional mask slipped back into place.

"That'll be Dr Whitman finishing with her patient," she said, her voice returning to its earlier careful tone. "She'll want to speak with you."

We walked back toward the reception area, passing several other rooms. Through one partially open door, I caught a glimpse of what looked like a small pharmacy—bottles and vials lined up on shelves, a scale for measuring doses, a locked cabinet that probably contained the more dangerous substances.

"Dr Whitman prepares her own medications?" I asked.

"She believes in precise dosing," Patricia replied. "Every patient is different. What works for one person might be harmful to another."

We reached the reception area just as Dr Whitman emerged from one of the treatment rooms, escorting a middle-aged man in an expensive suit. He looked dazed, uncertain, like someone who'd just woken up from a long sleep. She spoke to him in low, reassuring tones, then handed him off to a thin, nervous-looking man who'd been waiting in the reception area.

"James will take care of your next appointment, Mr Henderson," she said. "Remember what we discussed about letting the memories surface naturally."

The patient nodded vaguely and allowed himself to be led away by James Hartwell, the secretary. I watched them go, noting how Hartwell kept a helpful hand on the man's arm, as if he was used to dealing with patients who weren't quite steady on their feet.

Dr Whitman turned to me, and I saw the same composed professional demeanor she'd shown in my office, but there were shadows under her eyes that hadn't been there yesterday.

"Mr Collins, I trust Patricia has been helpful?"

"Very. I'd like to speak with you about some of your recent patients, particularly those who might have had access to confidential information."

She glanced around the reception area, then nodded toward her office. "Of course. Patricia, would you mind checking on the Henderson file? I want to make sure his medication levels are properly recorded."

Patricia nodded and disappeared into another room. Dr Whitman led me into her private office, a comfortable space with medical books lining the walls and a view of the garden through tall windows.

"I've been thinking about what you said yesterday," she began before I could speak. "About someone having access to confidential information. I've reviewed my files, and there are several patients who might have overheard conversations or seen documents they shouldn't have."

"Anyone in particular?"

She opened a filing cabinet and pulled out several folders. "Robert Ashford, of course. But also Margaret Sinclair—she's the wife of a Supreme Court judge. She was being treated for anxiety and depression following her husband's involvement in a controversial mining case. And there's David Chen, whose family owns several businesses in Chinatown. He was treated for opium addiction."

I made notes as she spoke, but I was thinking about what Patricia had said regarding patients who couldn't tell the difference between what really happened and what they thought happened. It seemed like a convenient explanation for someone who wanted to discredit a witness.

"Tell me more about Robert Ashford's treatment," I said. "What exactly was wrong with him?"

Dr Whitman closed the file and leaned back in her chair. "Robert came to me suffering from severe depression and anxiety following a mining accident. He felt responsible for the deaths of several workers and was experiencing what we call survivor's guilt. He was also having vivid nightmares and flashbacks."

"So you used hypnosis and pharmaceutical aids to help him?"

"Initially, yes. But Robert's case was more complex than I first realised. His memories of the accident were fragmented, confused. Sometimes he claimed the accident was deliberate, that someone had wanted those miners to die. Other times he insisted it was his fault, that he'd ignored safety warnings."

"Which version was true?"

She was quiet for a long moment, staring out the window at the garden. "That's the difficulty with traumatic memories, Mr Collins. The mind often distorts them to protect itself from unbearable truths. My job was to help Robert distinguish between his guilt and his actual responsibility."

"And how did you do that?"

"Through careful questioning under hypnosis, combined with mild sedatives to lower his psychological defenses. Gradually, we worked through his memories, separating fact from emotional reaction."

It sounded reasonable enough to a layman like me, but something in her tone suggested there was more to the story. "How did Robert react to this treatment?"

"At first, he seemed to improve. The nightmares decreased, and he was able to discuss the accident more calmly. But then..." She trailed off, her hands clasping and unclasping in her lap.

"Then what?"

"He began to question whether his memories were real. He claimed I was changing them, making him forget things he needed to remember. He became convinced that there was a conspiracy to cover up the truth about the mining accident."

"Was there?"

She looked at me sharply. "Mr Collins, I'm a doctor. My job is to help patients heal, not to determine legal guilt or innocence. If Robert believed there was a conspiracy, that was part of his psychological condition, not a reflection of reality."

But even as she said it, I could see doubt in her eyes. Whatever had happened to Robert Ashford, it had shaken her confidence in her own methods.

"When did he leave your care again?"

"About two months ago. He became increasingly agitated, claiming that I was working with his father to suppress his memories. He accused me of being part of the conspiracy." She stood up and walked to the window. "I tried to convince him that these were paranoid delusions, but he wouldn't listen. Finally, he stormed out, saying he was going to find proof of what really happened."

"And two weeks later he was dead."

"Yes." Her voice was barely audible. "When I heard about the accident, I wondered if I'd failed him somehow. If I'd pushed too hard, or not hard enough."

I closed my notebook and studied her face. She was holding something back, something that made her more frightened than guilty. In my experience, doctors who experimented with patients' minds usually had more confidence in their methods, not less.

"Dr Whitman, I need you to be completely honest with me. Was there anything unusual about Robert's treatment? Anything that might have given someone leverage over you?"

She turned from the window, and for a moment I saw past the professional mask to the frightened woman underneath.

"I may have...pushed the boundaries of accepted practice," she said quietly. "The pharmaceutical aids I used were stronger than I initially indicated. And the hypnosis sessions were more intensive than standard treatment protocols recommend."

"How much stronger?"

"Strong enough that Robert sometimes couldn't remember what we'd discussed in session. Strong enough that he had to be monitored for hours afterward to ensure he didn't harm himself while disoriented."

I felt that familiar tightness in my chest that came when a case started to show its real shape. "Dr Whitman, are you telling me that you were using mind-altering drugs on patients without their full consent?"

"I was trying to help them!" The words came out in a rush. 'Them,' not just Robert Ashford. "Robert was suffering, and conventional therapy wasn't working. I thought if I could help him access his suppressed memories, help him work through his guilt..."

"But instead you made him doubt his own mind."

She nodded, tears beginning to form in her eyes. "I realise now that I may have done more harm than good. But I never intended to hurt him. I was trying to heal him."

I stood up and walked to the door. "I need to speak with your secretary, James Hartwell. And I want to see Robert Ashford's complete file."

"Of course. But Mr Collins, please understand—I may have made mistakes in judgment, but I'm not a criminal. I'm a doctor who was trying to help a deeply troubled young man."

As I opened the door, I turned back to her. "Dr Whitman, in my experience, the road to hell is paved with good intentions. The question is whether someone else knew about your methods and decided to use them against you."

I left her office and went looking for James Hartwell, but my mind was already working through the implications of what I'd learned. Dr Whitman had been experimenting with dangerous treatments, possibly damaging her patients' ability to distinguish between reality and fantasy. Robert Ashford had become convinced there was a conspiracy, then died shortly after leaving her care.

The question was whether Robert's paranoid delusions had been the result of his treatment, or whether he'd stumbled onto something real that someone had wanted him to forget.

Either way, someone now had enough information about Dr Whitman's methods to destroy her career. And they were using it to extract £500—a sum that suggested this wasn't about money but about something much more valuable.

I found James Hartwell in a small office behind the reception area, hunched over a desk covered with patient files and appointment books. He looked up as I entered, and I saw the same nervous alertness I'd noticed in Patricia Mills.

"Mr Hartwell? I'm George Collins. Dr Whitman asked me to speak with you about the clinic's operations."

He was a thin man in his late thirties, perhaps, with prematurely gray hair and the sort of pallor that came from spending too much time indoors. His hands shook slightly as he closed the file he'd been working on.

"Yes, she mentioned you'd be coming by," he said, his voice carrying the educated accent of someone who'd come down in the world. "I'm not sure how much help I can be, but I'll answer what questions I can."

"Tell me about the patients who've left the clinic recently. Anyone depart under unusual circumstances?"

He glanced toward the door, then lowered his voice. "There have been several, actually. More than usual. Robert Ashford, of course, but also Margaret Sinclair and David Chen. And there were two others—a young woman named Sarah Fletcher and an older man, Professor Williams from the university."

"What made their departures unusual?"

"They all seemed...confused when they left. Disoriented. Like they couldn't quite remember why they'd been coming here in the first place." He hesitated, then added, "I keep detailed appointment records, and I noticed that all of them had been receiving what Dr Whitman calls 'intensive treatment' in the weeks before they left."

"Intensive treatment?"

"Longer sessions, usually two or three hours instead of the standard one hour. And they always seemed dazed afterward, like they'd been through something exhausting."

I made notes as he spoke, but I was thinking about the implications. Five patients receiving intensive treatment, all leaving confused and disoriented. It suggested a pattern that went beyond simple psychiatric therapy.

"Did any of them ever express concerns about their treatment?"

"Robert did, near the end. He came to me one day after a session, very agitated. He claimed that Dr Whitman was making him forget things, important things about the mining accident. He wanted to see his file, but of course I couldn't allow that without the doctor's permission."

"Did he say what specifically he thought he was being made to forget?"

James looked around nervously, then leaned closer. "He said something about the miners who died. He claimed they'd been trying to tell him something before the accident, something about dangerous conditions in the mine. But every time he tried to remember what it was, the memories would slip away."

"Did you believe him?"

"I didn't know what to believe. Robert was clearly disturbed, but he seemed so certain that something was being hidden from him." He paused, then added quietly, "And he wasn't the only one. Sarah Fletcher said something similar before she left. She claimed she was being treated for anxiety, but she couldn't remember what she was anxious about."

I closed my notebook and studied James's face. Like Patricia, he seemed to be walking a careful line between loyalty to his employer and concern about what he'd witnessed.

"One more question," I said. "Who has access to the patient files and treatment records?"

"Dr Whitman, of course. Patricia and myself. And Mrs Davies, the cleaning woman, but she only comes in to clean, not to work with files."

"Anyone else? Family members, visitors, other medical professionals?"

"No one unauthorized. Dr Whitman is very strict about confidentiality." He hesitated, then added, "Though I should mention that Charles Ashford, Robert's father, came by several times while his son was in treatment. He seemed very concerned about Robert's progress."

"Did he ever have access to Robert's file?"

"Not officially. But he did meet privately with Dr Whitman on several occasions. And he was very...insistent about being kept informed of his son's condition."

I thanked James and left the clinic, my mind working through what I'd learned. Dr Whitman had been using dangerous experimental treatments that left patients confused and disoriented. Several patients had departed under unusual circumstances, all claiming their memories were being manipulated. And Charles Ashford, Robert's father, had been closely involved in monitoring his son's treatment.

The pieces were beginning to form a picture, but it wasn't the simple blackmail case I'd initially expected. Someone knew about Dr Whitman's experimental methods and was using that knowledge to apply pressure. But whether the blackmailer was seeking justice or concealment remained to be seen.

As I walked back toward the tram stop, I found myself thinking about broken seams again. Dr Whitman's clinic was certainly a link in something larger, but I was beginning to suspect that the link extended far beyond the leafy streets of Woollahra.

The next step was to meet Charles Ashford and learn more about the mining accident that had started this whole chain of events. Something told me that the real story lay not in the psychiatric clinic, but in the dark tunnels beneath the coal mines of the Illawarra.

And if Robert Ashford had been right about a conspiracy, then someone had gone to great lengths to make sure he never remembered what he'd discovered down in those tunnels where five miners had died.

~ Chapter 3 ~

I decided to take the train to the Blue Mountains rather than drive. The locomotive to Katoomba wound through the foothills of the Blue Mountains like a steel snake climbing toward clearer air. I'd caught the morning service from Central Station, watching Sydney's industrial sprawl give way to eucalyptus forests and sandstone cliffs that looked like they'd been carved by giants. The other passengers were mostly day-trippers heading up to escape Sydney's humidity, but I was traveling toward something considerably less pleasant than scenic views and mountain air.

Charles Ashford's estate occupied a ridge above Katoomba, commanding a view that stretched across the Jamison Valley to the distant peaks beyond. The house itself was built in the colonial style, all wide verandas and sandstone walls, designed to remind visitors that the Ashfords had been wealthy long enough to build something permanent. But there was something defensive about the way it sat on its hill, surrounded by high walls and formal gardens that kept the wild bush at bay.

The taxi dropped me at the front gate, where a brass plaque announced 'Ashford House - Private Property.' I walked up the gravel drive, noting the well-maintained grounds and the expensive motor cars parked in the circular drive. Whatever Charles Ashford's business dealings involved, they were profitable enough to support this kind of establishment.

A middle-aged woman in a black dress answered the door, her expression suggesting she'd been expecting someone considerably more respectable than a private detective from Sydney.

"Mr Collins? Mr Ashford is waiting for you in the library."

She led me through a hallway lined with hunting prints and family portraits, the sort of décor that announced old money and established position. The library was a large room dominated by floor-to-ceiling bookshelves and French doors that opened onto a terrace overlooking the valley. It was the kind of room designed for serious conversations between serious men.

Charles Ashford stood with his back to me, staring out at the view. He was a big man, probably in his sixties, with silver hair and the sort of bearing that suggested he was used to being the most important person in any room. When he turned to face me, I saw eyes that were intelligent and calculating, but also haunted by something that might have been grief or guilt.

"Mr Collins." His voice carried the authority of someone accustomed to giving orders and having them obeyed. "I understand you're investigating some matter involving my son's former psychiatrist."

I took the chair he indicated, noting how he remained standing, using his height to maintain psychological advantage. It was a businessman's trick, but one that suggested he was more concerned about this conversation than he wanted to admit.

"Dr Whitman is being blackmailed," I said simply. "She asked me to investigate. Your son's name came up in connection with her treatment methods."

Something flickered in his eyes—anger, perhaps, or pain. "Robert is dead, Mr Collins. Whatever happened in that woman's clinic, it can't be changed now."

"Maybe not. But someone thinks there's information worth extracting money for. I need to understand what that might be."

He walked to a sideboard and poured himself a whiskey, not offering me one. His hands were steady, but I could see the tension in his shoulders.

"What do you want to know about my son?"

"Tell me about the mining accident that led to his treatment."

Charles took a sip of his whiskey, then set the glass down with deliberate care. "Robert was supervising operations at our Wollongong mine. There was a cave-in in one of the tunnels. Five men died." He paused, his jaw tightening. "Robert felt responsible. He'd been pushing the men to increase production, and he blamed himself for their deaths."

"Was he responsible?"

"Accidents happen in mining, Mr Collins. It's a dangerous business. But Robert was young, idealistic. He couldn't accept that sometimes good men die for no reason except bad luck."

I made notes as he spoke, but I was watching his face more than listening to his words. There was something rehearsed about his explanation, as if he'd told this story before and refined it over time.

"How did Robert end up in Dr Whitman's care?"

"He was having nightmares, drinking too much. His mother was worried about him, so I arranged for him to see the best psychiatrist in Sydney." His voice hardened. "I thought she would help him get past his guilt and return to normal life. Instead, she filled his head with nonsense about suppressed memories and psychological trauma."

"What kind of nonsense?"

Charles walked back to the window, his reflection ghostlike in the glass. "Toward the end of his treatment, Robert became convinced that the mine accident wasn't accidental. He claimed that someone had deliberately caused the cave-in to kill those workers."

"Did you believe him?"

"I believed he was having a breakdown." He turned back to me, his eyes cold. "Dr Whitman's treatments had made him paranoid, suspicious of everyone around him. He couldn't tell the difference between reality and delusion."

"But you continued to monitor his treatment."

"I visited the clinic several times, yes. I wanted to ensure my son was receiving the proper care." He paused, then added, "I also wanted to make sure Dr Whitman understood the importance of helping Robert move past his guilt, not wallowing in it."

The phrasing was careful, diplomatic, but I caught the underlying threat. Charles Ashford was the sort of man who was used to getting what he wanted, and he'd made sure Dr Whitman knew it.

"Did Robert ever mention keeping a diary or journal during his treatment?"

The question hit him like a physical blow. His glass slipped from his fingers, crashing to the floor and spraying whiskey across the expensive carpet. For a moment, his composed mask slipped, and I saw raw fear in his eyes.

"I—he may have written things down. Robert was always writing, even as a child." He bent to pick up the glass shards, using the motion to hide his face. "But after his death, I cleared out his belongings. There was nothing worth keeping."

"Nothing? No personal papers, no journals, no letters?"

"Just the ravings of a sick mind." He stood up, his composure restored but his hands shaking slightly. "Mr Collins, I don't see how ancient history can help with Dr Whitman's current problems. Perhaps you should focus on more recent events."

I closed my notebook and stood up. "One more question, Mr Ashford. Where exactly did Robert die?"

"Eagle Rock, about five miles from here. He was staying at a boarding house in town, run by a Mrs Thompson I believe, trying to..." He trailed off, then began again. "He was trying to pull himself together after leaving Dr Whitman's care. He'd been drinking, went walking alone near the cliffs. The police said he slipped and fell."

"But you don't think it was suicide?"

"Robert was getting better," he said firmly. "He was starting to accept that the accident wasn't his fault. He wouldn't have killed himself just when he was beginning to heal."

It was an interesting choice of words, given that he'd just finished describing Robert as paranoid and delusional. But I kept that observation to myself.

"I'd like to see where he was staying," I said. "Talk to the people who knew him during his final weeks."

Charles walked me to the door, his businessman's courtesy restored but his eyes still wary. "Of course. Though I doubt you'll learn anything useful. Robert wasn't himself in those last weeks."

As I walked back down the gravel drive, I found myself thinking about the dropped glass and the fear I'd seen in Charles Ashford's eyes when I'd mentioned a potential diary. A successful businessman didn't react that way to casual questions about his dead son's personal effects.

The taxi I'd arranged was waiting at the gate, and I gave the driver the address of Mrs Thompson's boarding house in town. As we wound down the mountain road, I made notes about the conversation, but my mind kept returning to Charles Ashford's assertion that Robert had been getting better, that he wouldn't have killed himself.

In my experience, people who insisted too strongly on a particular version of events usually had reasons for wanting that version to be believed. The question was whether Charles Ashford was protecting his son's memory or protecting himself from something Robert had discovered.

Mrs Thompson's boarding house was a modest weatherboard building on a quiet street lined with similar establishments. The Blue Mountains had always attracted people who wanted to escape something—the city heat, failed businesses, inconvenient pasts. It was the sort of place where a troubled young man could disappear for a while and try to sort out his problems.

Mrs Thompson herself was a woman in her fifties with kind eyes and the sort of practical manner that suggested she'd seen enough of human nature not to be surprised by much. She led me into a small parlor decorated with antimacassars and family photographs.

"Poor Robert," she said when I explained my purpose. "Such a troubled soul. He'd been with me for about three weeks when it happened."

"What was he like during those weeks?"

"Quiet, mostly. He kept to himself, spent a lot of time writing in his room. Sometimes I'd hear him pacing the floor late at night, like he couldn't settle." She shook her head sadly. "He was a gentleman, always polite, but you could see the pain in his eyes."

"Did he ever talk about what was troubling him?"

"Not directly. But he'd ask strange questions sometimes. About the mining accident, about whether I thought someone could make you forget things you needed to remember." She paused, then added, "He seemed convinced that people were lying to him, that there was some kind of conspiracy."

"Did you believe him?"

"I thought he was sick, to be honest. The way he'd look at you sometimes, like he wasn't sure if you were real or not. But then..." She hesitated, glancing toward the window.

"Then what?"

"The night before he died, he came to me all excited. Said he'd finally remembered something important, something that would change everything. He was going to write it all down, make sure the truth came out."

A diary? "Did he say what he'd remembered?"

"Something about the men who died in the mine. He said they'd been trying to warn him about something, but he'd been too frightened to listen at the time." She looked at me with troubled eyes. "He seemed so hopeful, Mr Collins. Like he'd finally found the answer he'd been looking for."

"And the next day he was dead."

"Yes. They found him at the bottom of Eagle Rock around noon. Said he'd been drinking and lost his footing." She shook her head. "But I'd seen him that morning, and he was sober as a judge. Excited, but sober."

I made notes as she spoke, but I was thinking about the timing. Robert had remembered something important, planned to write it down, and died the next day. It was the kind of coincidence that made my old criminal instincts start humming.

"Mrs Thompson, did Robert leave any personal belongings behind?"

"His father came and collected everything the day after the funeral. Said he didn't want Robert's things sitting around, reminding people of the tragedy." She paused, then added quietly, "Though I did keep one thing. Seemed too sad to throw away."

She left the room and returned with a small notebook, the kind used for keeping appointments or brief notes. "I found this under his mattress when I was cleaning the room. Must have fallen down behind the bed frame."

I opened the notebook and found myself looking at what must have been Robert Ashford's handwriting. Most of the pages were blank, but the last few contained what appeared to be fragments of memory:

'The black seam—they said it was dangerous, but Father insisted...'

'Thompson knew about the supports. Said they wouldn't hold, but orders came from above...'

'They were trying to tell me something before the shift ended. About the inspection, about why it had to happen that day...'

'Dr W keeps making me forget. Every time I remember, she takes it away again. But I'm starting to remember between sessions...'

'The diary—I hid it where Father will never find it. The truth about the black seam...'

That word again—diary. The entries were fragmentary, incomplete, but they painted a picture of a man struggling to hold onto memories that someone was trying to make him forget. And they suggested that Robert's paranoid delusions might have been based on very real events.

"Mrs Thompson, do you know where Robert might have hidden something? Somewhere his father wouldn't think to look?"

She considered the question carefully. "He used to take long walks in the bush behind the house. Said it helped him think. There's an old mine shaft back there, abandoned years ago. He mentioned it once, said it reminded him of the accident."

I thanked her and asked for directions to the mine shaft. As I walked through the bush behind the boarding house, I found myself thinking about the notebook entries. Robert had mentioned hiding his diary somewhere his father wouldn't find it. If I was a young man trying to preserve evidence of a conspiracy, where would I hide it?

The abandoned mine shaft was exactly the sort of place a troubled young man might choose—isolated, symbolic, and unlikely to be searched by anyone looking for hidden documents. It was also the perfect place for someone to have an accident, if they were being followed by people who wanted to make sure certain information never came to light.

I found the shaft opening after twenty minutes of searching, partially concealed by scrub brush and marked by a rotting sign warning of dangerous conditions. The opening was narrow, barely wide enough for a man to climb down, but someone had been here recently. The brush had been disturbed, and I could see scuff marks on the rocks around the entrance.

Using a torch I had borrowed from Mrs Thompson, I peered down into the darkness. The shaft descended about twenty feet before opening into what appeared to be a small chamber. I could see evidence that someone had been down there—footprints in the dust, disturbed rocks, and what looked like scratch marks on the walls where someone had been searching.

Getting down into the shaft required some of the climbing skills I'd learned during my less legal career, but I managed to reach the bottom without breaking my neck. I spent twenty minutes searching every crack and crevice in the rock walls, but found nothing except evidence that someone else had been there before me.

Looked like someone had beaten me to Robert's hiding place.

I climbed back up to ground level, my mind working through the implications. The diary that Robert had mentioned in his notebook fragments—the one he'd claimed contained the truth about the black seam—was gone. Someone had found it first, someone who'd known enough about Robert's habits to search this abandoned mine shaft.

The question was when they'd taken it. Had Charles Ashford found it after his son's death, or had someone else been tracking Robert's movements during his final weeks? Either way, the diary was now in the hands of someone who understood its value.

I walked back toward Mrs Thompson's boarding house, thinking about the notebook fragments I'd found. Robert had been convinced that the mining accident was deliberate, that his father was involved in covering up the deaths of five workers. But without the diary, I had no proof beyond the paranoid ravings of a man whose mind had been compromised by experimental psychiatric treatments.

The irony wasn't lost on me. Robert Ashford had tried to preserve the truth about the mining accident, but his own mental state had been so damaged by Dr Whitman's treatments that no one would believe his accusations. The perfect cover-up—discredit the witness by destroying his ability to distinguish between reality and delusion.

I reached Mrs Thompson's boarding house as the afternoon shadows were lengthening. She was in her garden, tending to a bed of roses, and looked up as I approached.

"Did you find what you were looking for, Mr Collins?"

"Someone got there first," I said. "The hiding place had been searched, probably recently."

She nodded sadly. "I thought as much. After the funeral, I saw Charles Ashford's motor car parked near the old mine road. Figured he was collecting more of Robert's belongings. But there was someone else nosing around here that day now that I bring it to mind."

"Who?"

"A young lady. Dark hair, asking questions. Now what was her name...I'm sure it started with a P..."

My heart skipped a beat. "Did she have brown eyes?"

"Why yes, yes she did," Mrs Thompson said with a smile. "But I can't for the life of me recall her name."

It didn't matter. I felt pretty sure it was Dr Whitman's nurse, Patricia Mills. This was an interesting development.

"What questions did she ask?"

"About Robert, how he was, what he did, things like that. Claimed she was a friend of his trying to reconnect with his memory."

Like I said, interesting. This put a new slant on the entire case.

"Did Robert ever mention what he'd written in his diary?"

"Not directly. But the night before he died, he said something about having proof that would clear his name. Said the five men who died in the mine hadn't been victims of an accident—they'd been murdered to keep them quiet about something."

"Did you believe him?"

"I wanted to. Robert was a good man, Mr Collins, whatever his troubles were. But he'd been so confused those last weeks, mixing up past and present, claiming people were lying to him." She paused, then added quietly, "Though I will say this—he seemed more lucid that last night than he had in weeks. Like the fog had finally lifted."

I thanked her and walked back to the railway station, my mind working through the implications of what I'd learned. Robert Ashford had been convinced that the mining accident was deliberate murder, and he'd written evidence of this conspiracy in his diary. But now the diary was gone, and Robert was dead, and the only people who knew the truth were those who'd participated in covering it up.

The train back to Sydney gave me time to think through the case. Dr Whitman was being blackmailed by someone who knew about her experimental treatments and their connection to Robert's death. The blackmailer had demanded £500 and warned that "broken links would be exposed."

But what if the blackmailer wasn't seeking money? What if they were seeking justice for the dead miners, using the only weapon they had—the threat of exposing Dr Whitman's role in Robert's mental destruction? And Patricia Mills was up here asking questions about Robert and his habits.

The pieces were starting to fit together, but I still didn't know who had Robert's diary or what they planned to do with it. I did know that Charles Ashford was more than just a grieving father—he was a man who'd shown genuine fear when I'd mentioned his son's journal, and who'd been quick to remove all traces of Robert's final weeks. He was seen here after the funeral. So was Patricia Mills. Either could have taken the diary.

As the train pulled into Central Station, I found myself thinking about seams and broken links again. The blackmail note had used that metaphor deliberately, suggesting that someone understood how the conspiracy was constructed and where its weaknesses lay.

Tomorrow I would travel to Wollongong and investigate the mining accident that had started this chain of events. If Robert Ashford had been right about the deaths of those five miners, then the truth was still buried in the black seam where they'd died.

And if I was lucky, I might find it before whoever had Robert's diary decided to use it for their own purposes.

~ Chapter 4 ~

The train to Wollongong ran south through industrial suburbs that gradually gave way to dairy farms and eucalyptus forests. I'd caught the early morning service, watching the city's smokestacks fade into the distance as we approached the Illawarra coast. The other passengers were mostly miners and steelworkers heading to their shifts, men with calloused hands and the sort of wary eyes that came from working in places where a moment's inattention could cost you your life.

After returning from the Blue Mountains, I'd spent the evening reading newspaper accounts of the mining accident that had traumatized Robert Ashford. The reports were brief and sanitized—five men killed in a tunnel collapse at the Ashford mine, investigation ongoing, safety measures being reviewed. The kind of stories that filled space between advertisements without telling readers anything that might upset them over their morning tea.

But I'd learned enough from my criminal days, as well as my years as an investigator, to read between the lines. The accident had occurred three months ago, just days before a scheduled safety inspection. The dead miners had all been experienced workers, not the sort of men who would ignore obvious dangers. And the tunnel that collapsed had been known to have structural problems, though no official warnings had been issued.

The taxi from Wollongong station took me through streets that smelled of coal smoke and industrial chemicals. This was a working town, built around the mines and steelworks that provided employment for most of its residents. The buildings were functional rather than beautiful, designed by men who understood that profit margins mattered more than architectural elegance.

The Ashford mine sat on a hillside underneath the towering Mt. Keira and overlooking the town, its headframe and machinery buildings marking the spot where men descended into darkness every morning. A sign at the entrance read "Ashford Mining Company—Safety First," but the irony wasn't lost on me. The same company that proclaimed its commitment to safety had allowed five men to die in a tunnel that likely should have been closed weeks earlier.

The mine office was a corrugated iron building that looked like it had been thrown together in an afternoon. I found the shift supervisor, Bill Crawford, in a small office cluttered with production reports and safety manuals. He was a man in his fifties with graying hair and the kind of steady manner that suggested he'd seen enough mining accidents to know how quickly things could go wrong underground.

"Mr Collins? You said on the telephone you wanted to know about the accident." He gestured for me to sit in a wooden chair that had seen better days. "Not much to tell that wasn't in the newspapers and reports."

"I'm investigating some matters related to Robert Ashford's death. I understand he was supervising operations when the accident occurred."

Crawford's expression darkened. "Poor bastard. He took it hard, losing those men. Blamed himself for something that wasn't his fault."

"What exactly happened that day?"

Crawford pulled out a manila folder and spread several documents across his desk. "We were working the black seam on the third level. It's a rich vein of coal, but the geology is tricky. The rock above it has a tendency to shift, especially when you're blasting close to the fault line."

He showed me a rough diagram of the mine layout, pointing to a section marked with red ink. "This is where the accident happened. The tunnel was about two hundred feet from the main shaft, following the coal seam as it angled down into the mountain."

"Had there been any warnings about the stability of that section?"

"Some." Crawford's voice was carefully neutral. "Old Tom Thompson, one of the men who died, had mentioned that the support timbers were creaking more than usual. Said he could hear the rock shifting at night when the mine was quiet."

"Did you report his concerns to management?"

"I mentioned it to Robert. He said he'd look into it, but..." Crawford shrugged. "Production quotas were tight that month. We were behind schedule because of equipment problems, and there was pressure from above to keep the coal moving."

I made notes as he spoke, but I was thinking about the notebook fragments I'd found at Mrs Thompson's boarding house. Robert had written about Thompson's warnings, about orders from above to keep working despite safety concerns.

"Tell me about the morning of the accident."

Crawford's face grew grim. "The shift started at six, same as always. The men were working on extending the tunnel face, using controlled blasts to break up the coal seam. Everything seemed normal until about ten o'clock."

"What happened then?"

"The first blast went off as planned. But when they set the second charge, something went wrong. The whole tunnel face collapsed, bringing down about fifty tons of rock and coal." He paused, then added quietly, "The five men working that section didn't have a chance."

"Was there any warning? Any sign that the tunnel was unstable?"

"Thompson had been nervous all morning. Kept checking the support timbers, measuring the gap between the roof and the beams. Just before the second blast, he tried to call a halt, said the rock was moving too much."

"But the blast proceeded anyway?"

"Like I said, Robert was under pressure to meet the production schedule. He overruled Thompson's concerns." Crawford's voice was heavy with regret. "It was a judgment call, and it turned out to be the wrong one."

I studied the mine diagram, noting the proximity of the collapsed tunnel to the main shaft. "Was there any investigation into the cause of the collapse?"

"The mining inspector came down from Sydney a few days later. He concluded that it was an accident, caused by unstable geology and the natural hazards of mining." Crawford paused, then added, "Though he did note that the tunnel should have been closed weeks earlier for safety reasons."

"And what happened to his report?"

"Filed away somewhere in the Mines Department, I suppose. These things happen in mining, Mr Collins. The rock doesn't always behave the way the engineers predict."

There was something in Crawford's tone that suggested he wasn't entirely satisfied with the official explanation. I pressed him further.

"You said Thompson was nervous that morning. Did he say anything specific about his concerns?"

Crawford hesitated, then pulled out a worn notebook from his desk drawer. "Tom kept a record of safety issues, things he thought should be reported to management. He showed me this the night before the accident."

The notebook was filled with Thompson's careful handwriting, documenting problems with support timbers, water seepage, and unusual rock movement in the black seam tunnel. The final entry, dated the day before the accident, was underlined in red ink:

"Third level tunnel showing signs of imminent collapse. Support timbers cracking under pressure. Recommend immediate closure until proper shoring can be installed. Rock movement increasing with each blast."

"Did you show this to Robert?"

"I tried to. But he was dealing with a lot of pressure from his father about production quotas. Said we couldn't afford to close the tunnel with the safety inspection coming up."

The timing was starting to make sense. The safety inspection had been scheduled for the week after the accident, and the Ashford mine was already behind on production. Closing the tunnel would have made it impossible to meet the quotas that Charles Ashford had set for his son.

"Who else knew about Thompson's concerns?"

"The other miners in his crew. They'd been talking about it for weeks, debating whether to refuse to work that section." Crawford's voice grew bitter. "But jobs are hard to come by in this economy. Men with families can't afford to be too particular about working conditions."

"Did any of them actually refuse to work the tunnel?"

"Three of them did, the morning of the accident. Said they'd rather face disciplinary action than risk their lives in an unstable tunnel." He paused, then added, "Those three men are still alive."

I made careful notes about the men who'd refused to work that day, thinking about the chain of decisions that had led to the accident. Robert Ashford had been caught between his father's demands for production and his workers' legitimate safety concerns. When he'd chosen to prioritize production, five men had died.

"Mr Crawford, was there any suggestion that the accident might not have been an accident at all? That it was a deliberate—"

His reaction was immediate and visceral, cutting me off. "What do you mean, deliberate?"

"Someone who wanted to eliminate the miners who'd been complaining about safety conditions. Someone who knew the tunnel was unstable and chose that moment to trigger a collapse."

Crawford stared at me for a long moment, then closed Thompson's notebook and put it back in his desk drawer. "That's a serious accusation, Mr Collins. You'd need proof before making that kind of claim."

"I'm not making any claims. I'm asking whether it's possible."

"Anything's possible in a mine. But why would anyone want to kill five good men?"

"To prevent them from testifying to safety inspectors about the dangerous conditions in the black seam tunnel."

Crawford's face went pale. "You think someone caused the accident to cover up the safety violations?"

"I think it's worth considering. The timing was convenient —just days before the inspection, eliminating the witnesses who could have testified about the dangerous conditions."

"But Robert was supervising that day. He wouldn't have been involved in murdering his own men."

"Maybe not. But someone with authority over Robert might have given him orders that he didn't fully understand. Someone who knew that the tunnel was unstable and chose that moment to insist on meeting production quotas."

Crawford sat back in his chair, his mind working through the implications. "Charles Ashford was here that morning. Came down to check on production progress, said he wanted to make sure we were ready for the safety inspection."

"Did he visit the tunnel face?"

"He went down to the third level with Robert. They were discussing the blasting schedule, how to maximize coal extraction before the inspection." Crawford paused, then added quietly, "Charles was very insistent that the work continue on schedule, despite the safety concerns."

"Did he know about Thompson's warnings?"

"Robert told him about the support timber problems. Charles said they couldn't afford delays, that the inspection was too important to risk falling behind on production."

The pattern was becoming clearer. Charles Ashford had known about the safety problems in the black seam tunnel, but had insisted that production continue anyway. When the tunnel collapsed, killing five men who could have testified about the dangerous conditions, the safety inspection found no witnesses to corroborate the warnings that had been ignored.

"Mr Crawford, do you still have access to the production records for that day?"

He pulled out another file and spread the documents across his desk. "These show the blasting schedule, the tonnage extracted, and the crew assignments for each shift."

I studied the records, noting that the five men who died had all been assigned to the most dangerous section of the tunnel. The men who'd refused to work that day had been reassigned to safer areas, while replacement workers had been brought in to fill the gaps.

"Who made these crew assignments?"

"Robert did, following instructions from his father. Charles wanted the most experienced miners working the black seam, said it was too important to trust to inexperienced workers."

"So the five men who died were specifically chosen for that assignment?"

"They were the best men for the job," Crawford said defensively. "But yes, they were specifically assigned to work the tunnel face that day."

The implications were chilling. Charles Ashford had known about the safety problems, had insisted that production continue despite the warnings, and had specifically assigned the five most vocal safety critics to work the most dangerous section of the tunnel. When the inevitable collapse occurred, the men who could have testified about the unsafe conditions were dead.

"Mr Crawford, did Robert ever talk about the accident afterward? About what he remembered from that day?"

"He was devastated. Kept saying he should have listened to Thompson's warnings, should have closed the tunnel despite the production pressure." Crawford's voice grew sad. "The guilt was eating him alive. He'd come to the mine at night sometimes, just sitting in his car outside the gate, staring at the headframe."

I closed my notebook and studied Crawford's face. He was a man who'd spent his career in the mines, who understood the dangers that miners faced every day. But he was also beginning to understand that the accident that had killed five of his men might have been something more sinister than simple negligence.

"Mr Crawford, if someone wanted to investigate the circumstances of the accident more thoroughly, would you be willing to cooperate?"

"If it would help get justice for those five men, yes. They were good workers, good men. Their families deserve to know the truth about what happened to them."

"What about the other miners? The ones who refused to work that day, and the ones who survived the accident?"

"They'd talk to you, I think. Most of them have been wondering why management was so insistent on maintaining production despite the obvious dangers."

I thanked Crawford and arranged to meet with some of the surviving miners later that afternoon. As I walked back toward the town center, I found myself thinking about the chain of events that had led to the accident. Charles Ashford had known about the safety problems but had insisted on maintaining production. He'd specifically assigned the five most vocal safety critics to work the most dangerous section of the tunnel. And when the collapse occurred, the men who could have testified about the unsafe conditions were dead.

The perfect murder, disguised as an industrial accident. And when Robert Ashford had begun to suspect the truth, he'd been sent to Dr Whitman for treatment that had destroyed his ability to distinguish between reality and paranoid delusion.

But Robert had fought back, keeping a secret diary that documented what he'd discovered about the conspiracy. Now that diary was in the hands of someone who understood its value, someone who was using it to apply pressure to the one person who could expose the truth about Robert's mental destruction.

The question was whether that person was seeking justice for the dead miners or simply exploiting their deaths for personal gain. Either way, the truth about the black seam was finally beginning to surface, and I intended to make sure it saw the light of day before anyone else died to protect it.

The afternoon interviews with the surviving miners confirmed what I'd begun to suspect. The five men who'd died had all been vocal critics of the safety conditions in the black seam tunnel. They'd been planning to submit a formal complaint to the mining inspector about the dangerous working conditions, and they'd been specifically assigned to work the tunnel face on the day of the accident.

More disturbing was the revelation that Charles Ashford had visited the mine that morning, ostensibly to check on production progress. But several miners had seen him in close conversation with the blast foreman, discussing the placement of charges for maximum coal extraction. The timing of the explosion, just as the safety critics were working the most dangerous section of the tunnel, was beginning to look less like accident and more like murder.

As I rode the train back to Sydney, I couldn't help but think once again about the notebook fragments I'd found at Mrs Thompson's boarding house. Robert had written about his father's insistence on maintaining production despite safety warnings, about orders from above to keep working the black seam despite the obvious dangers.

But Robert had also written about his own role in the tragedy, about the guilt that had driven him to seek psychiatric treatment. He'd been caught between his father's demands for production and his workers' legitimate safety concerns. When he'd chosen to prioritize production, five men had died.

The irony was bitter. Robert Ashford had been both victim and perpetrator, manipulated by his father into making the decision that had killed five men, then psychologically destroyed when he'd begun to understand the truth about what had happened.

Now someone had Robert's diary, someone who understood its value as evidence of the conspiracy that had killed five miners and driven a young man to suicide. The blackmail note to Dr Whitman had mentioned 'broken seams of trust'—a metaphor that suggested the blackmailer understood how the conspiracy was constructed and where its weaknesses lay.

As the train pulled into Central Station, I mulled over the entirety of the case again. I needed to learn more about Patricia Mills. Who was she, what's her story? I made a mental note to do so soon. The mining accident had been the first seam in a chain of events that had led to Robert's psychological destruction and eventual death. But somewhere in that chain was a weak link, a point where the conspiracy could be exposed and the truth about the black seam finally brought to light.

The question was whether I could find that weak link before the people who'd killed six men decided to eliminate another witness to their crimes.

~ Chapter 5 ~

The morning after my return from Wollongong, I sat in my Castlereagh Street office with the pieces of the puzzle spread across my desk like fragments of a broken mirror. Each piece reflected part of the truth, but I needed to see the whole picture before I could understand how deep the conspiracy ran.

I'd spent the night reviewing my notes, drawing connections between the mining accident, Robert's psychological treatment, and the blackmail of Dr Whitman. The pattern that emerged was darker than simple industrial negligence or medical malpractice. It was a carefully orchestrated series of crimes designed to eliminate witnesses and destroy evidence.

The telephone rang, interrupting my thoughts. Tom Majors' voice came through the receiver, gruff and businesslike.

"Magpie, I've got some information about that mining accident you asked me to look into. Can you come down to headquarters?"

Twenty minutes later, I was sitting in Majors' office at the station on Phillip Street, listening to what his contacts in the Mines Department had uncovered. The official file on the Ashford mine accident was thinner than it should have been, but it still contained enough information to confirm my suspicions.

"The mining inspector who investigated the accident was a man named Hal Fitzpatrick," Majors said, consulting his notes. "He's been with the department for fifteen years, good reputation, thorough investigator. But his report on the Ashford accident was unusually brief."

"What did he conclude?"

"Accidental collapse due to geological instability. He noted that the tunnel should have been closed weeks earlier, but he didn't pursue the question of why it hadn't been." Majors paused, then added, "What's interesting is that Fitzpatrick retired two weeks after filing his report. Bought a nice house in Manly, well beyond what his government salary should have allowed."

"Someone bought his silence."

"Looks that way. But there's more. I contacted the families of the five miners who died. They all received compensation payments that were significantly higher than the standard amounts. Enough to keep them comfortable and quiet."

I made notes as Majors spoke, thinking about the systematic way the conspiracy had been constructed. Charles Ashford hadn't just caused the accident—he'd made sure that everyone who might investigate it or complain about it was either dead or bought off.

The scope of the cover-up was impressive. Charles Ashford had anticipated every possible source of trouble and neutralized it with a combination of money, intimidation, and murder. The five miners who'd died had been the only ones who couldn't be bought or relocated.

"Tom, I need you to look into something else. The psychiatric treatment that Robert Ashford received from Dr Whitman. I think his father arranged it specifically to destroy Robert's ability to expose the truth about the accident."

"You think the psychiatrist was part of the conspiracy?"

"I think she was coerced into it. The same way the mining inspector was bought off, the same way the surviving miners were relocated. Charles Ashford had a system for dealing with potential problems."

Majors leaned back in his chair, his expression grim. "If you're right, we're looking at conspiracy to commit murder, bribery of public officials, and God knows what else. But we'll need solid evidence before we can move against someone like Charles Ashford."

"I'm working on it. But I need protection for Dr Whitman. If the blackmailer decides to go public with what they know, she could be in danger from the same people who killed the miners."

"I've already arranged everything since your last telephone call. But Magpie, be careful. If Ashford was willing to kill five miners to cover up safety violations, he won't hesitate to eliminate anyone else who threatens to expose him."

I left the police station with more questions than answers, but at least I had confirmation that my suspicions about the mining accident were justified. The systematic nature of the cover-up suggested that Charles Ashford had been planning something like this for a long time, waiting for the right opportunity to eliminate the witnesses who threatened his mining operations.

My next stop was the State Library, where I spent the afternoon researching Charles Ashford's business history and the broader context of mining operations in the Illawarra region. What I found painted a picture of a man who'd built his fortune on a foundation of calculated ruthlessness, with a pattern of accidents and likely cover-ups stretching back over two decades.

The Ashford Mining Company had been founded in 1920, when Charles had purchased several played-out mines in the Illawarra region. Using new extraction techniques and a workforce willing to accept dangerous conditions in exchange for steady wages, he'd transformed the failing operations into profitable enterprises.

But his success had come at a cost. The newspaper archives contained numerous references to mining accidents at Ashford operations, each one followed by reports of generous compensation payments to the families of the dead. The pattern was consistent—accidents occurred just before safety inspections, eliminating workers who'd been complaining about dangerous conditions.

The black seam tunnel where the recent accident had occurred was part of a mining complex that Charles had acquired in 1928. The previous owner had closed the tunnel after geological surveys showed it was too unstable for safe operations. But Charles had reopened it anyway, using experimental support techniques that increased production while reducing safety margins.

The records showed that Robert Ashford had been placed in charge of the black seam operations just six months before the accident. His father had been training him to take over the family business, teaching him that profit margins were more important than worker safety.

But Robert had been different from his father. The reports from other mining operations suggested that he'd been genuinely concerned about worker safety, that he'd tried to implement improvements that would have reduced accident rates. His father had overruled most of these initiatives, claiming they were too expensive and unnecessary.

The conflict between father and son had been building for months before the accident. Robert had been caught between his natural compassion for the workers and his father's demands for increased production. When the crisis came, he'd chosen to follow his father's orders, and five men had died as a result.

The guilt had driven Robert to seek psychiatric treatment, but even that had been manipulated by his father. Charles Ashford had chosen Dr Whitman specifically because her experimental techniques could be used to suppress Robert's memories of the accident and prevent him from exposing the truth.

The picture that emerged from the archives was of a man who'd spent twenty years perfecting the art of industrial murder. Profit—massive profit—above all else. Charles Ashford had discovered that mining accidents were the perfect cover for eliminating troublesome workers, and he'd used that knowledge to build a business empire on a foundation of calculated death.

By the time I left the library, I understood the full scope of the conspiracy. The mining accident hadn't been a single act of criminal negligence—it had been the culmination of a systematic campaign to silence anyone who threatened to expose the dangerous conditions in the Ashford mines.

The evening was spent reviewing my notes and drawing connections between the various elements of the case. The blackmail of Dr Whitman was just one strand in a web of corruption that stretched from the coalface to the corporate boardroom to the psychiatric clinic.

Someone had been working patiently to gather evidence about the conspiracy, someone with access to Robert's treatment records and knowledge of the mining accident. The references to 'broken seams of trust' in the blackmail note suggested that the blackmailer understood exactly how the conspiracy was constructed and where its weaknesses lay.

My thoughts that night drifted back to Patricia Mills, the clinic nurse who'd been asking questions about Robert Ashford before his death. Her nervousness during our initial meeting, her detailed knowledge of the experimental treatments, her access to confidential patient records—and her visit to the Blue Mountains—all pointed to her involvement in the blackmail scheme.

But there was something else, something that suggested her motivation wasn't simple greed. The precision of the blackmail note, the specific references to medical ethics and patient confidentiality, indicated that she understood the moral implications of what Dr Whitman had done. This wasn't just about money—it was about justice.

The question was whether Patricia Mills was seeking justice for the dead miners or simply exploiting their deaths for personal gain. Either way, she was in possession of evidence that could expose the full extent of Charles Ashford's crimes, and that made her a target for the same people who'd killed six men to protect their secret.

Tomorrow I would need to confront both Dr Whitman and Patricia Mills, to understand their roles in the conspiracy and to ensure that the truth about the black seam finally came to light. But tonight, I needed to make sure that Tom Majors was prepared to move against Charles Ashford when the time came.

Because the black seam of corruption that Charles Ashford had created was beginning to collapse, and anyone caught in its path was in mortal danger. The chain of events that had started with five dead miners was about to reach its conclusion, and I intended to make sure that justice was finally served for all the victims of the Ashford conspiracy.

~ Chapter 6 ~

The morning rain drummed against the windows of Dr Whitman's clinic as I waited in the reception area, watching the secretary James Hartwell sort through appointment cards with the methodical precision of a man who'd learned to find comfort in routine. The events of the past few days had crystallized into a pattern of conspiracy and murder that reached from the coalface of Wollongong to the consulting rooms of Woollahra, and I knew the time had come to confront the doctor with what I'd discovered.

Patricia Mills glanced up from her nursing station as I entered, her expression carefully neutral, but I caught the flicker of recognition in her eyes. She knew why I was here, and her slight nod toward Dr Whitman's office told me that the doctor was expecting me as well.

"Mr Collins," Dr Whitman's voice was strained as she opened her office door. "Please, come in. I believe we have much to discuss." I noted that Patricia had picked up her coat and was appearing to leave as I entered the doctor's office.

The office looked different in the gray morning light—less authoritative, more vulnerable. The diplomas on the walls and the leather-bound medical texts seemed like props in a play rather than symbols of professional competence. Dr Whitman herself looked as though she'd aged years in the few days since our first meeting, her careful composure replaced by the hollow-eyed exhaustion of someone who'd been carrying a terrible secret for too long.

"Doctor, I've spent the past few days investigating the circumstances surrounding Robert Ashford's death and the mining accident that preceded it." I settled into the chair across from her desk, noting how she flinched at the mention of the mine. "I think it's time you told me the truth about his treatment."

She was quiet for a long moment, staring at her hands folded in her lap. When she finally spoke, her voice was barely above a whisper.

"I never intended for any of this to happen. You have to believe that, Mr Collins. When I first agreed to treat Robert, I thought I was helping a young man overcome the trauma of witnessing a terrible accident."

"But it wasn't just trauma, was it? Robert had discovered something about that accident, something that his father needed to keep buried."

Dr Whitman's composure cracked, and I saw the tears she'd been holding back begin to flow. "Charles Ashford came to see me two weeks after Robert began treatment. He said his son was having dangerous delusions, that he was convinced the mining accident had been deliberate murder."

"And you believed him?"

"At first, yes. Robert was clearly disturbed by what he'd witnessed. He was having nightmares, flashbacks, episodes where he couldn't distinguish between reality and his guilt-ridden memories." She paused, dabbing at her eyes with a handkerchief. "Charles said the delusions were becoming more elaborate, that Robert was constructing conspiracy theories to avoid accepting responsibility for the deaths of his workers."

I made notes as she spoke, but I recalled the notebook fragments I'd found at Mrs Thompson's boarding house. Robert hadn't been delusional—he'd been documenting the truth about his father's crimes.

"What exactly did Charles Ashford ask you to do?"

"He wanted me to use my experimental techniques to help Robert accept reality, to stop him from pursuing these dangerous fantasies about deliberate murder." Her voice grew steadier as she continued. "He said Robert was threatening to go to the authorities with his suspicions, that it would destroy the family's reputation and possibly lead to criminal charges based on nothing more than a traumatized young man's paranoid delusions."

"So you agreed to treat Robert specifically to suppress his memories of the accident?"

"I thought I was treating a patient suffering from survivor's guilt and trauma-induced paranoia. Charles provided me with detailed accounts of Robert's behavior, documentation of his increasingly erratic statements about the accident." She pulled a file from her desk drawer and handed it to me. "These are copies of the reports Charles gave me about Robert's condition."

I studied the documents, noting the clinical language used to describe Robert's 'delusional episodes' and his 'paranoid fixation' on the idea that the mining accident had been deliberate. The reports painted a picture of a young man whose guilt over the miners' deaths had driven him to construct elaborate conspiracy theories to avoid accepting responsibility.

"But these reports were fabricated, weren't they? Charles Ashford was manipulating you just as he'd manipulated the mining inspector and the miners' families."

Dr Whitman's face crumpled. "I didn't realise it at the time. Charles was so convincing, so concerned about his son's mental health. He had documents, witness statements from mine workers who supposedly confirmed Robert's erratic behavior."

"What methods did you use to treat Robert?"

"I employed a combination of hypnosis and experimental drug therapy, techniques I'd been developing for treating severe trauma cases, as I've previously explained to you." Her voice grew clinical, as though distancing herself from the emotional weight of what she was describing. "The goal was to help Robert reconstruct his memories of the accident in a way that would allow him to accept the reality of what had happened without being overwhelmed by guilt."

"In other words, you were trying to make him forget what he'd discovered about the deliberate nature of the accident."

"I was trying to help him accept that the accident was exactly that—an accident, not a deliberate act of murder. The techniques I used were designed to reduce the emotional intensity of traumatic memories, to allow patients to process difficult experiences without being paralyzed by guilt or paranoia."

I thought about the fragments of Robert's notebook, the careful documentation of his father's role in the conspiracy. "But Robert fought back, didn't he? He found ways to record his real memories, to document what he'd discovered about the mining accident."

"Yes." The word came out as a whisper. "Despite the treatments, Robert continued to maintain that the accident had been deliberate. He kept a diary, which he hid from me and from his father. He would write in it between sessions, documenting what he called his 'real memories' as opposed to the 'false memories' he said I was trying to implant."

"Did you ever read this diary?"

"No, but I knew he was keeping it. Sometimes he would refer to it during our sessions, claiming it contained evidence that would prove his father's guilt." She paused, then continued more quietly. "I thought it was another manifestation of his paranoid delusions. I even used the existence of the diary as part of the treatment, trying to convince him that his need to document these supposed conspiracies was actually a symptom of his inability to accept reality."

The cruel irony was obvious. Robert had been desperately trying to preserve the truth about his father's crimes, while his own psychiatrist had been systematically destroying his ability to distinguish between reality and delusion.

"When did you begin to suspect that Charles Ashford might have been lying to you?"

Dr Whitman was quiet for a long moment, staring out the rain-streaked window. "About a month before Robert's death, I began to notice inconsistencies in the reports Charles was providing. Details about Robert's behavior that didn't match what I was observing during our sessions."

"What kind of inconsistencies?"

"Charles claimed that Robert was becoming increasingly violent and unpredictable, that he was making threats against mine workers and officials. But during our sessions, Robert was withdrawn and depressed, not aggressive. He seemed more frightened than angry."

"Did you confront Charles about these discrepancies?"

"I tried to discuss them with him, yes, but he became very defensive. He said I didn't understand the full scope of Robert's condition, that his son was skilled at presenting different personalities to different people." She paused, then added quietly, "He also reminded me of how much my reputation depended on the success of Robert's treatment."

The threat was subtle but clear. Charles Ashford had been using Dr Whitman's professional ambitions against her, just as he'd used financial pressure against the mining inspector and the miners' families.

"What happened during Robert's final weeks of treatment?"

"He became increasingly agitated, claiming that his father was planning to have him committed to an asylum to prevent him from exposing the truth about the mining accident." Her voice grew shaky. "I thought it was another paranoid delusion, but Charles had mentioned the possibility of long-term institutional care if Robert's condition didn't improve."

"Did you believe that Robert was genuinely disturbed enough to require institutionalization?"

"No," she said firmly. "Despite the experimental treatments, despite the memory suppression techniques, Robert remained fundamentally rational. Depressed and guilt-ridden, but not psychotic or dangerous." She paused, then added, "But Charles had legal authority as his father, and he'd been building a documented case for involuntary commitment."

"Is there anything else you can tell me about this case, Dr Whitman? Anything at all?"

The doctor took a deep breath. She was finally willing to tell all. "The night before Robert's death, he came to see me at my home. He was agitated, frightened, but also more lucid than I'd seen him in weeks." She took a shuddering breath. "He told me that he'd discovered evidence proving that his father had deliberately caused the mining accident to eliminate witnesses who could testify about unsafe working conditions."

"What kind of evidence?"

"He claimed to have found documents showing that his father had known about the structural problems in the tunnel, that he'd specifically assigned the five men who died to work the most dangerous section despite their safety concerns." She paused, then added, "He also said he'd discovered that several mine officials had been bribed to suppress safety reports."

All this I had already discerned. "Did you believe him?"

"I thought it was another elaborate delusion, more evidence of his inability to accept the reality of what had happened." Her voice grew bitter. "I tried to convince him to return to treatment, to allow me to help him work through these latest fantasies."

"But he refused?"

"He said he was going to the authorities the next morning, that he had enough evidence to prove his father's guilt in the murders of five men." She was crying again. "He begged me to examine my own records, to see how I'd been manipulated into participating in a conspiracy to destroy his memories."

"And then he killed himself?"

"The next morning, I received a telephone call saying that Robert had been found dead at the base of Eagle Rock in the Blue Mountains. The official cause was listed as accidental death, but..." She trailed off, unable to continue.

"But you suspected suicide?"

"I suspected that Robert had realised the futility of fighting against such a comprehensive conspiracy. He'd been systematically isolated from everyone who might have believed him, and his own psychiatrist had been working to destroy his ability to trust his own memories."

The picture was becoming clear. Robert had been caught in an impossible situation—the only witness to multiple murders, but systematically discredited by the very people who were supposed to help him. His father had used Dr Whitman's professional expertise to destroy Robert's credibility, while building a legal case for involuntary commitment if other methods failed.

"Dr Whitman, I need to ask you about the blackmail note you received. Do you have any idea who might have sent it?"

She hesitated, then pulled the note from her desk drawer and handed it to me. "I've been thinking about it constantly since our first meeting. The references to 'broken seams of trust' suggest someone who understands the full scope of what happened to Robert."

"Someone with access to his diary?"

"Possibly. The note mentions that phrase—that's almost exactly the phrase Robert used to describe what he thought I was doing to him." She paused, then added, "He said I was breaking the seam of trust between doctor and patient, that I was using my position to destroy rather than heal."

"Who else knew about Robert's diary?"

"I mentioned it to Charles during our consultations, though I emphasised that I considered it a symptom of Robert's delusional thinking." She looked stricken. "I also discussed it with Patricia Mills, my nurse. She was helping me document Robert's progress, and I thought she should be aware of all aspects of his condition."

The mention of Patricia Mills caught my attention. According to everything I'd thus far discovered, she was particularly interested in Robert's treatment and had visited the Blue Mountains not long after his death.

"Did Patricia Mills ever express any concerns about Robert's treatment?"

"She seemed genuinely concerned about his welfare, more so than I would have expected from a nurse." Dr Whitman paused, thinking. "She often asked detailed questions about the treatment methods, about whether the memory suppression techniques were really in Robert's best interest."

"What did you tell her?"

"I explained that the treatments were experimental but necessary, that Robert's delusional thinking posed a danger to himself and others." She was quiet for a moment. "But Patricia seemed skeptical, as though she didn't entirely believe my explanations."

"And she had access to all your medical files," I said more to myself than to the doctor. "I saw Patricia leaving just as I entered your office."

"That's odd. She doesn't have the afternoon off."

The implications were beginning to crystallize. Patricia Mills had been present during Robert's treatment, had access to his medical records, and had expressed concerns about the experimental techniques being used. She would have been in a position to understand exactly how Robert's memories were being manipulated, and why.

"Dr Whitman, I need to ask you a direct question. Are you willing to admit that you participated in a conspiracy to suppress Robert's memories of his father's crimes?"

She was quiet for a long moment, staring at her hands. When she finally spoke, her voice was firm despite the tears.

"Yes. I allowed myself to be manipulated into using my professional skills to destroy a patient's ability to distinguish between reality and delusion. I participated in a conspiracy that ultimately drove Robert to suicide." She looked up at me, her eyes red but determined. "I'm prepared to testify about what I did, about how Charles Ashford used me to silence his son."

"Even though it will destroy your career?"

"My career is already destroyed. The blackmail note makes that clear—someone has evidence of what I did, and they're going to use it whether I cooperate or not." She paused, then added quietly, "At least this way, Robert's death might serve some purpose. At least the truth about what happened to him might finally come to light."

"Are you prepared to face criminal charges for your role in the conspiracy?"

"If that's what it takes to get justice for Robert and for the miners who died, yes." Her voice was steady now, filled with the resolve of someone who'd finally decided to stop running from the truth. "I've spent weeks trying to rationalize what I did, trying to convince myself that I was helping Robert rather than destroying him. But the facts are clear—I used my professional skills to participate in a conspiracy that led to the death of my patient."

I closed my notebook and studied Dr Whitman's face. She was a broken woman, but she was also a woman who'd finally found the courage to confront the truth about her actions. Her testimony would be crucial in exposing the full scope of Charles Ashford's conspiracy, but it would also require a degree of moral courage that few people possessed.

"Dr Whitman, I've already arranged for police protection for you. I have a friend on the force who should be in contact with you about that shortly. If Charles Ashford was willing to kill five miners and manipulate his own son into suicide, he won't hesitate to eliminate anyone who threatens to expose him."

"I understand. But Mr Collins, there's something else you need to know." She pulled out a final file from her desk. "These are copies of all my records related to Robert's treatment. I've been keeping them as insurance, in case Charles ever tried to deny his role in the conspiracy."

"What do they show exactly?"

"They document every conversation I had with Charles about Robert's condition, every report he asked me to prepare, every technique he suggested I use to suppress Robert's memories." She handed me the file. "They prove that Charles was directing Robert's treatment from the beginning, that he was using me as a tool to destroy his son's ability to expose the truth about the mining accident."

The file was thick, filled with detailed notes about Charles Ashford's involvement in his son's psychiatric treatment. The documents painted a picture of a man who'd orchestrated every aspect of Robert's psychological destruction, using his knowledge of medical procedures and legal requirements to build an impenetrable case against his own son.

"Dr Whitman, along with your testimony, this is evidence of conspiracy to commit murder. Charles Ashford didn't just manipulate you—he systematically destroyed Robert's mental health to prevent him from exposing the truth about the mining accident."

"I know. And I'm prepared to testify about every detail of what he did." She paused, then added quietly, "It's the least I can do for Robert, and for the miners who died because of his father's greed."

As I prepared to leave, I found myself thinking about the seam of events that had led to this moment. The mining accident had been the first link in a series of crimes that had stretched from the coalface to the psychiatric clinic. Charles Ashford had systematically eliminated everyone who threatened to expose his crimes, using murder, bribery, and psychological manipulation to protect his secret.

But it was all starting to finally break down. Dr Whitman's testimony would expose the medical conspiracy that had driven Robert to suicide, while the evidence I'd gathered in Wollongong would prove that the mining accident had been deliberate murder.

The question now was whether I could bring Charles Ashford to justice before he realised that his carefully constructed conspiracy was collapsing around him. Because if I was right about the scope of his crimes, he wouldn't hesitate to eliminate anyone who stood in his way—including a psychiatrist who'd finally found the courage to tell the truth about what she'd done.

As I walked through the rain toward my car, I thought about Robert Ashford's diary, somewhere in the hands of someone who understood its value as evidence. The blackmail note had mentioned "broken links" and "chains of trust"— metaphors that suggested the sender understood exactly how the conspiracy had been constructed and where its weaknesses lay.

Tomorrow I would need to confront Patricia Mills about her role in the case, to understand whether she was seeking justice for Robert and the miners or simply exploiting their deaths for personal gain. But tonight, I had a different task. I needed to contact Tom Majors and confirm his involvement in protecting Dr Whitman.

Because the black seam of corruption that Charles Ashford had created was finally beginning to collapse, and anyone caught in its path was in mortal danger. The truth about the mining accident and Robert's death was finally coming to light, and I intended to make sure that justice was served for all the victims of the Ashford conspiracy.

The rain continued to fall as I drove through the darkening streets of Sydney, thinking about seams and broken links, about the connection between industrial murder and medical malpractice, about the price of truth in a world where powerful men could destroy lives with impunity.

But sometimes, if you were patient and persistent, you could find the weak link in even the strongest seam. And I was beginning to think that I'd finally found the key to bringing down Charles Ashford's empire of corruption and murder.

~ Chapter 7 ~

The next morning found me parked outside Patricia Mills' modest flat in Balmain, watching the early shift workers make their way to the docks through the grey dawn light. I'd spent the night reviewing everything I knew about the clinic nurse, piecing together the fragments of information that suggested she was more than just an innocent bystander in the Robert Ashford case.

Her address had been easy to obtain from the clinic records, and a few telephone calls to neighbours had confirmed that she lived alone in a small flat above a bakery, keeping to herself and rarely speaking about her work. But it was what I'd discovered about her background that made me certain she was the person I was looking for.

Patricia Mills had been born Patricia Henley in Wollongong, the daughter of a coal miner who'd worked the dangerous seams of the Illawarra region for thirty years. Her brother Michael had died in the Ashford mine accident three months ago, one of the five men crushed when the black seam tunnel collapsed. She'd taken the job at Dr Whitman's clinic just two weeks after the funeral, using false references and a fabricated employment history to gain access to Robert Ashford's treatment.

The picture was becoming clearer. Patricia Mills wasn't just a nurse who'd stumbled onto evidence of a conspiracy—she was a woman seeking justice for her brother's murder, using her position at the clinic to gather evidence about the cover-up that had followed the mining accident.

I waited until I saw her leave for work, then followed her Ford sedan through the morning traffic toward Woollahra. Instead of going directly to the clinic, she stopped at a small café in Paddington, where she sat alone at a corner table, nursing a cup of tea and reading a newspaper. But her attention wasn't on the news—she was watching the street, waiting for someone.

After twenty minutes, she folded the newspaper and walked to a nearby post office, where she collected mail from a private box. Among the letters was a manila envelope that she opened carefully, studying the contents before placing them in her handbag. The envelope bore the return address of a law firm in the city, and I suspected it contained information about the mining accident investigation.

I followed her to the clinic, where she parked in her usual spot and entered through the staff entrance. But instead of going directly to her nursing station, she stopped at Dr Whitman's office, where the two women had a brief, intense conversation. Through the window, I could see Patricia gesturing emphatically while Dr Whitman shook her head, their discussion clearly heated.

The conversation ended abruptly when Patricia noticed me watching from the reception area. She walked over to where I was standing, her expression carefully controlled but her eyes betraying the tension she was feeling.

"Mr Collins. You're here again? Is there something specific you need?"

"I need to speak with you privately, Miss Mills. Or should I say, Miss Henley?"

The use of her real name had the desired effect. Her carefully maintained composure cracked, and I saw the fear and anger that she'd been keeping hidden beneath her professional demeanor.

"I don't know what you're talking about."

"I think you do. Your brother Michael died in the Ashford mine accident three months ago. You took this job specifically to investigate Robert Ashford's treatment, to gather evidence about the conspiracy that killed your brother."

She glanced around the reception area, noting that James Hartwell was watching our conversation with obvious interest. "Not here. Meet me at the Botanical Gardens in an hour. Near the harbour bridge end."

She walked away without waiting for my response, leaving me to wonder whether she would actually show up or use the time to disappear. But I had the feeling that Patricia Mills—Patricia Henley—was tired of running from the truth, tired of carrying the burden of her brother's death alone.

An hour later, I found her sitting on a bench overlooking the harbour, watching the morning ferries carry commuters to their offices in the city. She'd changed from her nursing uniform into a simple dress that made her look younger, more vulnerable. But her eyes held the same determined anger I'd seen at the clinic.

"You're right," she said without preamble. "My name *is* Patricia Henley, and Michael *was* my brother. He died in that tunnel because Charles Ashford was too greedy to care about worker safety."

"Why didn't you go to the police with your suspicions?"

"What suspicions? That a mining accident wasn't really an accident?" She laughed bitterly. "The official investigation concluded that it was caused by geological instability. The mining inspector filed his report and retired to a nice house in Manly. The families received compensation payments that kept them quiet."

"But you knew it was more than that."

"Michael wrote to me every week. In his last letter, he told me about the safety problems in the black seam tunnel, about how the miners were being forced to work in conditions they knew were dangerous." She pulled a folded letter from her handbag. "He said Thompson and the others were planning to file a formal complaint with the mining inspector, that they had evidence of negligence that would shut down the operation."

I read the letter, noting Michael Henley's careful documentation of the safety violations and his concern about the company's refusal to address the problems. The letter was dated five days before the accident, and it painted a picture of workers who knew they were risking their lives but felt powerless to change their circumstances.

"Did you show this to the authorities?"

"I tried. But the mining inspector had already filed his report, and the police said it was a civil matter for the Mines Department." She took the letter back, folding it carefully. "Everyone kept telling me that accidents happen in mining, that grief was making me see conspiracies where none existed."

"So you decided to investigate on your own."

"I decided to find out what really happened to my brother. And when I learned that Robert Ashford was receiving psychiatric treatment for trauma related to the accident, I knew I had to get close to him."

"You fabricated your credentials to get the job at Dr Whitman's clinic?"

"I have genuine nursing training, but I used false references to hide my connection to the mining accident. I needed to be in a position to observe Robert's treatment, to understand what he knew about what had happened."

The plan showed a degree of sophistication that impressed me. Patricia had recognized that Robert Ashford was the key to exposing the truth about the mining accident, and she'd positioned herself to gather evidence about his treatment and condition.

"What did you discover about Robert's treatment?"

"As you've already discovered, that Dr Whitman was using experimental techniques to suppress his memories of the accident. She was systematically destroying his ability to distinguish between reality and delusion." Patricia's voice grew angry. "Robert knew the truth about what his father had done, but the treatments were making him doubt his own memories."

"Did you try to help him?"

"I tried to document what was happening to him, to preserve evidence of the memory suppression techniques." She paused, then added quietly, "But I also tried to help him maintain his grip on reality. I would talk to him between sessions, encouraging him to write down what he really remembered before the treatments could affect his recall."

"You encouraged him to keep a diary?"

"I suggested it as a way to track his progress, but Robert understood the real purpose. He was fighting a desperate battle to preserve his memories, and the diary was his weapon in that fight."

The pieces were falling into place. Patricia hadn't just been observing Robert's treatment—she'd been actively working to sabotage it, helping him maintain his ability to remember the truth about the mining accident.

"Did you ever read Robert's diary?"

"Not while he was alive. I respected his privacy, and I thought the diary would be more valuable as evidence if I could honestly say I hadn't influenced its contents." She was quiet for a moment. "But after his death, I went to his lodgings and retrieved it from its hiding place before anyone else could find it."

"So it *was* you that beat me to that mine and took the diary from it."

"Yes. Mrs Thompson, his landlady, told me where Robert used to like taking his walks. I found it hidden there and made sure to preserve it."

"What did the diary contain?"

Patricia reached into her handbag and pulled out a small leather notebook, its pages filled with Robert's careful handwriting. "Everything. His memories of the mining accident, his father's role in causing it, the names of the officials who were bribed to suppress the investigation."

I studied the diary, noting the meticulous way Robert had documented his discoveries about the conspiracy. The entries were clear and rational, showing no signs of the delusional thinking that Dr Whitman had described in her reports.

"Robert wasn't suffering from paranoid delusions, was he?"

"He was suffering from guilt and depression, but his memories of the accident were completely accurate. The treatments were making him doubt his own perceptions, but the diary shows that he never stopped believing in the truth of what he'd witnessed."

"And you used this diary as the basis for your blackmail note to Dr Whitman?"

Patricia's expression hardened. "I wasn't blackmailing her for money. I was trying to force her to confront the truth about what she'd done to Robert."

"But you did demand payment."

"I demanded that she confess her role in the conspiracy and provide evidence that could be used to prosecute Charles Ashford." She paused, then added, "The money was just to make it look like ordinary blackmail, to prevent her from realizing the real purpose of the note."

"What was the real purpose?"

"To force her to admit that she'd been manipulated into participating in a conspiracy to suppress evidence of murder. I needed her testimony to corroborate what Robert had written in his diary."

The strategy was clever. By disguising her demand for justice as simple blackmail, Patricia had protected herself from charges of more serious crimes while still applying pressure to the one person who could expose the medical conspiracy.

"Did you know that Dr Whitman was acting under duress when she treated Robert?"

"I suspected it. Charles Ashford visited the clinic regularly, and I could see the effect his presence had on Dr Whitman. She was frightened of him, eager to please him." Patricia's voice grew bitter. "But I also knew that she was using her professional skills to destroy a patient's mental health. Whatever her motivations, she was participating in something evil."

"Are you prepared to testify about what you witnessed at the clinic?"

"I've been preparing for that possibility since the day I took the job. I'm not going to let my brother's death—all the victims—go unchallenged. They all deserve justice."

I studied Patricia's face, seeing the pain and anger that had driven her to construct such an elaborate plan for justice. She'd risked everything to gather evidence about the conspiracy, using her position at the clinic to document the systematic destruction of Robert's mental health.

"Patricia, you do realise that what you've done is technically illegal? The forged credentials, the theft of the diary, the blackmail note—any of those could result in criminal charges."

"I know. But what else could I do? The official investigation was a whitewash, the police weren't interested in pursuing it, and the only witness was being systematically silenced through psychiatric manipulation." She paused, then added quietly, "Sometimes you have to choose between legal and right." She looked out at the harbour, where the morning ferries were carrying their passengers to offices and shops across the city. "I've been living with the weight of their deaths for months. At least this way, their deaths might serve some purpose."

I found myself admiring Patricia's courage and determination, even as I recognized the dangerous position she'd placed herself in. She was prepared to face the legal consequences of her actions if it meant getting justice for the victims. Then, a thought occurred to me.

"Patricia, I need to ask you about something else. Do you know anything about the other mining accidents at Ashford operations? The pattern of accidents followed by generous compensation payments?"

"Michael mentioned them in his letters. He said the older miners talked about previous accidents, about how workers who complained about safety conditions had a tendency to be assigned to the most dangerous jobs." She paused, then added, "They called it 'the black seam treatment'—getting assigned to work the most dangerous coal seams until you either quit or got killed."

"Did Michael think the previous accidents were deliberate?"

"He thought they were too convenient to be coincidental. Safety complainers would get assigned to dangerous work, and then accidents would happen that eliminated the complainers while leaving the compliant workers unharmed."

The pattern was becoming clear. Charles Ashford had been systematically eliminating troublesome workers for years, using mining accidents as the perfect cover for murder. The five men who'd died in the black seam tunnel had been just the latest victims in a long campaign of industrial murder.

"You'll need police protection. I can arrange that for you. But first, I need to know whether you've told anyone else about the evidence you've gathered."

"No one. I've been working alone, afraid to trust anyone with what I'd discovered." She paused, then asked, "Do you think we have enough evidence to prosecute Charles Ashford?"

"With your and Dr Whitman's testimonies, the doctor's files, and the evidence I've procured from my own investigation, yes. But we need to move carefully. Charles Ashford is a powerful man with resources and connections. If he realises that his conspiracy is being exposed, he'll try to eliminate anyone who can testify against him."

"What do you want me to do?"

"Continue working at the clinic as if nothing has changed. Don't let anyone know that you've spoken to me about the case. And if Charles Ashford contacts you directly, let me know immediately."

Patricia nodded, understanding the dangers involved. She'd spent months gathering evidence about the conspiracy, and she wasn't going to jeopardize the investigation by acting prematurely.

"Mr Collins, there's something else you should know. Yesterday, after you left the clinic, Charles Ashford came to see Dr Whitman. They had a long conversation in her office, and she looked terrified when he left."

"Did you hear what they discussed?"

"Not all of it, but I heard him mention something about 'loose ends' and 'final solutions.' He seemed to be warning her about something."

The timing was ominous. Charles Ashford had visited Dr Whitman shortly after I'd confronted her about the conspiracy, and secured her cooperation, suggesting that he was already aware that his carefully constructed secret was beginning to unravel.

"I have a friend on the force who will be in touch with you about police protection. Follow his instructions to the letter and I'll be in touch. Be careful."

As I walked back to my car, I found myself thinking about the chain of events that had led to this moment. The mining accident had been the first link in a chain of crime that had stretched from the coalface to the psychiatric clinic. But Patricia Henley had been working patiently to document every link in that chain, gathering evidence that could finally bring Charles Ashford to justice.

The question now was whether we could move fast enough to prevent him from eliminating the witnesses who could testify against him. Because if I was right about the scope of his crimes, Charles Ashford wouldn't hesitate to kill again to protect his secret.

But Patricia had given me something more valuable than evidence—she'd given me hope that justice was still possible, even when the official system had failed. Her courage and determination reminded me that sometimes the most important battles were fought not by police or prosecutors, but by ordinary people who refused to accept that power could triumph over truth.

The black seam of corruption that Charles Ashford had created was finally being exposed, and I intended to make sure that every victim of his crimes finally received the justice they deserved. The seam of murder and conspiracy that had started with five dead miners was about to be broken, and the truth about the black seam would finally see the light of day.

~ Chapter 8 ~

The telephone call came early the next morning, Charles Ashford's voice cutting through the quiet of my Castlereagh Street office like a blade through silk. I'd been expecting it, had spent the night preparing for it, but the cold authority in his tone still sent a chill down my spine.

"Mr Collins, I believe you have something that belongs to me."

"That depends on what you think I have, Mr Ashford."

"Don't play games with me, Detective. My sources tell me you've been asking questions about my son's death, about the unfortunate accident at my Wollongong operation." His voice carried the casual menace of a man accustomed to getting his way through intimidation. "I think it's time we had a conversation about the limits of your investigation."

I'd been hoping he would make contact, but I'd also been dreading it. Charles Ashford was a man who'd killed at least six people to protect his secret, and I had no illusions about what he was capable of doing to preserve his empire of corruption.

"I'm always willing to discuss my cases with interested parties, Mr Ashford. When and where would you like to meet?"

"Tonight. Eight o'clock. My estate in the Blue Mountains—you know the address." The line went quiet for a moment, then he added, "Come alone, Mr Collins. And bring whatever evidence you think you've gathered about my business affairs. I'm prepared to make you a generous offer for your discretion."

The threat was implicit but clear. Charles Ashford was offering me a choice between money and death, between corruption and justice. It was the same choice he'd offered the mining inspector, the same choice he'd given Dr Whitman, the same choice he'd presented to everyone who'd discovered the truth about his crimes.

"I'll be there, Mr Ashford. Eight o'clock sharp."

"Excellent. I look forward to our discussion."

The line went dead, leaving me staring at the telephone and thinking about the trap I was walking into. Charles Ashford hadn't survived thirty odd years in the mining business by being careless about loose ends, and I had no doubt that he was planning to eliminate me just as he'd eliminated everyone else who'd threatened to expose his secret.

I had all the proof needed to end this case already, to achieve the kind of justice all the victims deserved and then some. This meeting would merely be the icing on the cake. I spent the morning making arrangements with Tom Majors, outlining the plan we'd developed for the evening's confrontation. The police would be positioned around the

Ashford estate, hidden in the thick bush that surrounded the property. But they would stay back unless I gave them a specific signal, allowing Charles Ashford to reveal his crimes without realizing that every word was being recorded.

The plan was dangerous, but I wanted to hear Charles Ashford admitting to everything. Such rich bastards had to know they didn't rule the world, that their evil would ultimately have consequences. I was realistic enough to know that was almost never the case, but I was determined to at least make this rich scumbag see the truth.

I called Patricia Henley at the clinic and determined both her and Dr Whitman's safety. Police in plain clothes were watching over them already, and they proceeded in their lives as per normal for the present. I advised her of the situation with Charles Ashford for later that evening. She wanted to come along. I thought it was a terrible idea.

"Patricia, I need you to promise me something. If the situation goes wrong tonight, if Charles Ashford tries to eliminate me, you'll make sure Dr Whitman's testimony reaches the authorities."

"I promise. But I also need you to promise that you'll make him admit what he did to Michael and the others. I need to know that their deaths weren't meaningless."

"I'll do everything I can," I told her. "One way or another, justice for your brother—for everyone—is coming."

I hung up and took a little while to gather my thoughts. The afternoon passed slowly as I reviewed the evidence I'd gathered about the mining conspiracy, preparing for the confrontation that would either see Charles Ashford confessing to his crimes or cost me my life. The diary Patricia had recovered from Robert's lodgings, Dr Whitman's records of the medical conspiracy, the testimony of the miners who'd survived the accident—all of it pointed to a systematic campaign of murder and cover-up that had claimed at least six lives. But I wanted Ashford to admit to it all. My sense of justice for the little guy would not settle for anything less.

But, as Tom had told me, even with the evidence we had already collected, a powerful lawyer may be able to get Ashford off—or secure a lighter sentence somehow—making the procuring of this confession even more important. I had to go through with it.

As the sun began to set behind the Blue Mountains, I loaded my revolver and checked the recording device Tom had provided. The plan was simple but dangerous: I would meet with Charles Ashford, allow him to explain his version of events, and try to provoke him into admitting his role in the mining murders. If everything went according to plan, the police would have enough evidence to arrest him for conspiracy to commit murder.

But plans had a way of going wrong, especially when dealing with men like Charles Ashford. He'd survived thirty years in a brutal industry by being ruthless and calculating, and I had no doubt that he'd prepared for every contingency. The question was whether I could outmaneuver him, whether I could turn his own arrogance and cruelty against him.

This time I wouldn't leave the journey up to the vagaries of public transport. I took my car. The drive to the Blue Mountains took two hours through winding roads that climbed steadily into the cool air of the highlands. The Ashford estate occupied the same commanding position on a ridge overlooking the Jamison Valley as per my previous visit. This time, its imposing picture of wealth and power proved even more menacing than before.

I parked my car in the circular drive and noted the black sedans positioned at strategic points around the property. Charles Ashford had brought reinforcements, just as I'd expected. The question was whether Tom Majors and his men had been able to position themselves effectively in the surrounding bush.

The front door was opened by a man I didn't recognize— tall, broad-shouldered, with the careful movements of someone accustomed to violence. He searched me thoroughly, removing my revolver and the recording device Tom had provided. But he missed the backup device I'd hidden in my shoe, the small microphone that would capture every word of the conversation to come.

"Mr Collins. Welcome again to my home." Charles Ashford emerged from the shadows of the entrance hall, his voice carrying the same cold authority I'd heard on the telephone. "I trust your journey was pleasant?"

"Pleasant enough, Mr Ashford. Though I have to say, the reception committee seems a bit excessive for a simple business discussion."

"In my experience, Mr Collins, it's always wise to be prepared for unexpected developments." He gestured toward a study lined with hunting trophies and mining equipment. "Shall we proceed to my office? I believe we have much to discuss."

The study was a monument to Charles Ashford's career— photographs of mining operations, awards from industry organizations, maps showing the extent of his coal holdings throughout the Illawarra region. But it was the framed photograph on his desk that caught my attention: a younger Charles Ashford standing with a group of miners, all of them smiling at the camera with the easy camaraderie of men who worked dangerous jobs together.

"My first crew at the Wollongong operation," Charles said, noting my interest. "Good men, all of them. Most of them dead now, of course—mining is a dangerous business."

"Some more dangerous than others, I imagine."

"Indeed." He settled behind his desk, his eyes never leaving my face. "Now, Mr Collins, I understand you've been investigating my son's death and the unfortunate accident at my mine. I'm curious about what you think you've discovered."

This was the moment I'd been preparing for, the chance to draw Charles Ashford into admitting his crimes. But I also knew that one wrong word, one sign that I was trying to trap him, could end with my body buried somewhere in the Blue Mountains wilderness.

"Your son Robert was receiving psychiatric treatment for trauma related to witnessing the mining accident, which is common knowledge. But I've also learned that he believed the accident was deliberate, that you had arranged for those five miners to die."

Charles was quiet for a moment, his expression unreadable. Then he began to laugh, a sound that was more chilling than any threat.

"Poor Robert. Even after all of Dr Whitman's efforts, he never could accept the reality of what happened." He leaned forward, his voice taking on a confidential tone. "My son was a sensitive boy, Mr Collins. Too sensitive for the mining business, too guilt-ridden to understand that sometimes difficult decisions must be made for the greater good."

"What kind of difficult decisions?"

"The kind that prevent unnecessary suffering, that protect the livelihood of hundreds of workers and their families." His voice grew harder. "Those five miners were planning to file safety complaints that would have shut down the entire operation. Hundreds of men would have lost their jobs, their families would have suffered, all because of the paranoid fears of a few troublemakers."

"So you arranged for them to die?"

"I arranged for them to be assigned to work that suited their talents. If they were foolish enough to ignore safety protocols, if they were careless enough to trigger a tunnel collapse, that was their own responsibility."

The admission was chilling in its casual cruelty. Charles Ashford was confessing to multiple murders with the same tone he might use to discuss the weather, as though the deliberate killing of five men was simply a routine business decision.

"And Robert discovered what you'd done?"

"Robert discovered what he thought I'd done. But his guilt over the accident, his inability to accept that dangerous work sometimes results in tragic consequences, drove him to construct elaborate conspiracy theories." Charles's voice grew bitter. "He was convinced that I was some kind of monster, that I'd deliberately murdered five men to protect my business interests."

"Hadn't you?"

"I'd made a difficult decision based on the greater good. Sometimes, Mr Collins, individual lives must be sacrificed to protect the welfare of the community." He paused, then added quietly, "Robert never understood that principle. He was too weak, too sentimental to grasp the realities of industrial leadership."

"So you arranged for him to receive psychiatric treatment to suppress his memories?"

"I arranged for him to receive the help he needed to overcome his paranoid delusions. Dr Whitman's experimental treatments were designed to help Robert accept reality, to free him from the guilt and conspiracy theories that were destroying his mental health."

"Even if those conspiracy theories were true?"

Charles was quiet for a long moment, his eyes studying my face with the calculating gaze of a predator evaluating prey. "Mr Collins, I think you misunderstand the nature of truth. Truth isn't simply a matter of what happened—it's a matter of what serves the greater good, what protects the interests of the community."

"And if the community's interests require the death of troublesome miners?"

"Then those deaths serve a higher purpose than the individual lives that are lost." His voice was completely calm, as though he were discussing a philosophical principle rather than confessing to murder. "The mining industry employs thousands of men throughout New South Wales. The economic stability of entire communities depends on the continued operation of mines like the one at Wollongong."

"So you killed five men to protect your business interests?"

"I made a decision that preserved the jobs and livelihood of hundreds of families. If five troublemakers had to die to protect the welfare of the community, then their deaths served a noble purpose."

The confession was complete, but I could see in Charles's eyes that he was beginning to realise he'd said too much. The casual tone was fading, replaced by the cold calculation of a man who'd spent his life eliminating threats to his empire.

"Mr Collins, I trust you understand the sensitive nature of what we've discussed tonight. I'm prepared to offer you substantial compensation for your discretion in this matter."

"What kind of compensation?"

"Enough to ensure your comfortable retirement from the private investigation business. A generous payment for services rendered, with the understanding that your investigation into my son's death and the mining accident has reached its conclusion."

The offer would have been tempting for a dishonest man, or a desperate one. I was neither. But I could see the trap he was laying. Charles Ashford had no intention of allowing me to leave his estate alive, regardless of whether I accepted his bribe or not. I was the last loose end in a conspiracy that had already claimed six lives, and he was preparing to eliminate me just as he'd eliminated everyone else who'd threatened to expose his crimes.

"That's a generous offer, Mr Ashford. But I'm afraid I can't accept it."

"I was hoping you wouldn't say that, Mr Collins."

The words were spoken with quiet regret, but I could see the cold satisfaction in his eyes. Charles Ashford had been planning this moment from the beginning, had lured me to his estate specifically to eliminate the threat I posed to his carefully constructed empire of corruption.

"You see, Mr Collins, I've spent many years building my business, creating an industrial empire that provides employment and economic stability for thousands of people. I'm not going to allow a small-time shamus to destroy everything I've accomplished."

"Even if it means committing more murders?"

"Even if it means protecting the greater good from the destructive influence of misguided idealism." He stood up, moving toward the window that overlooked the dark valley below. "Robert never understood that principle. He was too weak to grasp the realities of power, too sentimental to make the difficult decisions that leadership requires."

"So you had him killed?"

"I had him treated for his mental illness. The fact that he chose suicide rather than accepting the reality of his situation was his own decision." Charles turned back to face me, his expression completely cold. "But you, Mr Collins, don't have the luxury of that choice."

The threat was explicit now, and I could see the hired gunmen moving into position around the study. Charles Ashford had played his hand, had revealed the full scope of his crimes, but he was also preparing to eliminate the only witness to his confession.

"Before you make any irreversible decisions, Mr Ashford, there's something you should know. The police have been listening to every word of our conversation."

"I don't think so, Mr Collins. My men searched you thoroughly, and they found the recording device the police obviously provided." He held up the small recorder I'd been carrying. "Did you really think I wouldn't anticipate such an obvious trick?"

"I thought you might anticipate the obvious tricks. That's why I brought backup."

I stamped my foot twice on the floor, activating the emergency signal that would bring Tom Majors and his men racing to the estate. But I also knew that it would take them several minutes to reach the house, and Charles Ashford's gunmen were already moving into position.

"An interesting bluff, Mr Collins. But I'm afraid it won't save you."

The sound of breaking glass came from the front of the house, followed by shouts and the sound of running feet. Tom Majors had positioned his men closer than I'd expected, and they were moving in fast to prevent Charles Ashford from eliminating the evidence of his crimes.

"Actually, Mr Ashford, it wasn't a bluff."

The study door burst open as Tom Majors and three constables rushed in, their revolvers drawn and ready. Charles Ashford's gunmen found themselves surrounded, caught between the police at the door and the windows they'd been using to watch the grounds.

"Charles Ashford, you're under arrest for conspiracy to commit murder and the deaths of five miners at your Wollongong operation."

But Charles wasn't finished. As Tom moved to place him in handcuffs, he broke away and ran toward the back of the house, crashing through a set of French doors. Tom and I raced after him, and quickly found ourselves in the garden. I took the lead, knowing that Ashford was heading for the thick bush that surrounded the estate, hoping to lose himself in the wilderness until he could find a way to escape.

The chase led through the manicured gardens and into the natural bushland that covered the ridge above the Jamison Valley. Charles Ashford was older than me but he clearly knew the terrain, and he moved through the dense scrub with the sure-footedness of a man who'd spent his younger days exploring these mountains.

But I'd grown up in the rough neighborhoods of Sydney, and I knew how to track quarry through hostile territory. I followed the sounds of his passage through the bush, the crack of breaking branches and the rustle of disturbed undergrowth that marked his desperate flight.

The pursuit led to a narrow ledge overlooking the valley, where Charles had stopped to catch his breath and plan his next move. He turned as I approached, his face wild with the desperation of a man who'd seen his carefully constructed empire crumble in a single evening.

"You've destroyed everything, Collins. Decades of work, thousands of jobs, the economic foundation of whole communities, this entire state." He was mad with egoism.

"I've exposed the truth about what you did to those miners, about what you did to your own son."

"Truth?" His laugh was bitter and desperate. "You think truth matters more than the welfare of the community? Of the state? You think the lives of five troublemakers were worth more than the jobs and security of thousands of people?"

"I think murder is murder, regardless of your insane justification."

"And I think you're a naive fool who doesn't understand the realities of power." He moved toward the edge of the ledge, his eyes never leaving my face. "But you won't live to see the consequences of what you've done."

He reached for something in his jacket—a gun, I quickly realised, as it came into brief view. But as he drew the pistol, his foot slipped on the loose rock at the edge of the precipice.

I lunged forward, trying to grab his hand, but it was too late. As Tom arrived at my side, Charles Ashford fell backward into the darkness of the valley, his scream echoing off the cliff walls until it was swallowed by the night.

The rest of Tom's men found us standing at the edge of the precipice, staring down into the black depths where Charles Ashford had fallen. The recording device in my shoe had captured every word of his confession, providing the evidence needed to prosecute his surviving associates and expose the full scope of the mining conspiracy.

"Did you get what you needed?" Tom asked, his voice quiet in the mountain stillness.

"I got his confession about the mining murders, about his role in driving Robert to suicide. Everything we need to bring guaranteed justice to the families of the victims."

"Charles Ashford paid the ultimate price," Tom said.

I looked down into the valley where his body lay broken on the rocks below. "Charles Ashford's death mirrored that of his son. A sad irony, perhaps. The black seam of corruption he created claimed him just like it claimed all the others."

As we walked back through the bush toward the estate, I couldn't help but think about the chain of events that had led to this moment once again. The mining accident had been the first link in a seam of crime that had stretched from the coalface to the psychiatric clinic to the mountain precipice where Charles Ashford had met his end.

But the seam was finally broken. The truth about the mining murders was exposed, Dr Whitman's testimony would reveal the medical conspiracy, and Patricia Henley would finally have the justice she'd sought for her brother and the other victims.

The black seam of corruption that had run through Charles Ashford's empire was finally sealed, and the light of justice could finally penetrate the darkness that had hidden his crimes for so long.

But as we reached the estate and began the long process of documenting the evidence, I knew that other seams of corruption would always exist, other powerful men who would sacrifice individual lives for their own interests. The battle for justice was never truly over—it simply moved from one battlefield to another.

The important thing was that this particular battle had been won, that the victims of Charles Ashford's greed had finally received the justice they deserved. The black seam had been exposed and sealed, and that was enough for now.

~ Chapter 9 ~

The morning sun was just beginning to filter through the Blue Mountains mist when Tom Majors and I made our way down the treacherous cliff face to where Charles Ashford's body lay broken on the rocks below. The fall had been nearly two hundred feet, and there was no question about the outcome. The man who had orchestrated the deaths of at least six people had finally paid the price for his crimes.

"Looks like he hit the ledge about halfway down," Tom observed, his voice echoing off the canyon walls. "Then bounced off into the main drop."

I knelt beside the body, noting the way Charles Ashford's limbs were twisted at impossible angles. His expensive suit was torn and bloodied, his face barely recognizable from the impact. But clutched in his right hand was the pistol he'd been trying to draw when he fell, the weapon he'd planned to use to silence me permanently.

"He was reaching for this when he lost his footing," I said, carefully extracting the gun from his death grip. "Another few seconds and he would have added my name to his list of victims."

Tom examined the weapon, noting the serial number that had been filed off. "Professional job. This wasn't something you'd buy at a regular gun shop."

"Charles Ashford was nothing if not thorough. He'd been planning to eliminate me from the moment he realised I was getting too close to the truth." I looked up at the cliff face we'd just descended, calculating the trajectory of the fall. "But his own greed and arrogance destroyed him in the end."

The recovery of the body took most of the morning, requiring specialized equipment and mountain rescue personnel. But by noon, Charles Ashford's remains were loaded into a police wagon for the journey back to Sydney, where the coroner would conduct the official examination.

Tom decided to join me in my car as we returned to Sydney. It felt good to have a friend alongside me. As we drove back through the winding mountain roads, I found myself thinking about the confession Charles had made before his death. The recording device hidden in my shoe had captured every word, providing irrefutable evidence of his role in the mining murders and the conspiracy to suppress Robert's memories.

"It was chilling to hear him describe the deaths of those men as serving 'the greater good,'" I said after a long period of silent thought.

"Men like Charles Ashford always find ways to justify their crimes," Tom replied. "They convince themselves that their actions serve some higher purpose, that individual lives don't matter compared to their grand designs."

"The recordings will be enough to prosecute his surviving associates—the mine supervisors who carried out the sabotage, the safety inspectors who were bribed to ignore the dangerous conditions, the officials who covered up the investigation."

"What about Dr Whitman?"

"She was acting under duress, threatened with professional and personal destruction if she didn't cooperate. The recordings prove that she was coerced into participating in the conspiracy."

I thought about the psychiatrist's anguished confession, her genuine remorse for what she'd been forced to do.

"She'll face disciplinary action from the medical board, but I doubt she'll be prosecuted criminally."

"And Patricia Henley?"

"She'll face charges for the forged credentials and the blackmail note, but any reasonable prosecutor will recognize that she was seeking justice for her brother's murder. I suspect she'll receive a suspended sentence, especially if she testifies against the surviving conspirators."

The drive back to Sydney gave me time to plan the next phase of the investigation. Charles Ashford's death had eliminated the central figure in the conspiracy, but the network of corruption he'd created would take months to fully unravel. Mine supervisors, safety inspectors, government officials—all of them would need to be questioned and, where appropriate, prosecuted.

But first, I needed to return to the clinic to collect Dr Whitman's testimony and ensure that she understood the further protection she would receive in exchange for her cooperation. The woman had been through enough trauma, and I wanted to make sure she felt safe enough to provide the detailed testimony that would be needed to convict the surviving conspirators.

I found Dr Whitman in her office, staring out the window at the clinic's grounds with the vacant expression of someone who'd seen her world collapse around her. She looked up as I entered, her eyes searching my face for some indication of what had happened since we last spoke.

"Mr Collins. I heard on the radio that there was some kind of incident at the Ashford estate. Is Charles...?"

"Charles Ashford is dead. He fell from a cliff while trying to escape arrest after confessing to the murder of five miners and the conspiracy to suppress his son's memories."

The relief that flooded her face was unmistakable. For months, she'd been living in fear of Charles Ashford's retaliation, terrified that he would destroy her career and her life if she refused to cooperate with his demands.

"Just like his son. Does that mean it's over? That I'm safe?"

"It means that Charles Ashford can never threaten you again. But there are still others involved in the conspiracy who will need to be prosecuted, and your testimony will be crucial to their conviction."

I explained the legal protections that would be available to her, the guarantees that she would face no criminal charges in exchange for her cooperation. She listened carefully, occasionally asking questions about the process and the timeline for the prosecutions.

"What about my medical license? My practice?"

"The medical board will conduct their own investigation, but I suspect they'll be more interested in preventing similar situations than in punishing a doctor who was coerced into participating in a conspiracy." I paused, then added, "Your reputation may be damaged, but you'll have the opportunity to rebuild it by helping to bring justice to the victims of

Charles Ashford's crimes. And who knows what the future will then hold?"

"And Patricia? I know now she was the one who sent the blackmail note."

"Patricia will face charges, but she'll also receive credit for her role in exposing the conspiracy. She risked everything to gather evidence about her brother's murder, and that will count in her favor."

Dr Whitman nodded slowly, beginning to understand that she had a chance to redeem herself by helping to expose the full scope of the conspiracy. "What do you need me to do?"

"I need you to prepare a detailed statement about Charles Ashford's coercion, about the specific techniques you used to suppress Robert's memories, about any other officials who were involved in the cover-up." I handed her a legal pad. "Write down everything you remember, no matter how insignificant it might seem. The prosecutors will need every detail to build their cases."

As Dr Whitman began writing, I again thought about the long chain of events that had led to this moment. Five miners had died in a tunnel collapse that had been deliberately caused to prevent them from exposing safety violations. Robert Ashford had discovered the truth about the murders and had been driven to suicide by psychiatric treatments designed to destroy his memories. Charles Ashford had died while trying to eliminate the last witnesses to his crimes.

But the seam of corruption that had started with industrial murder was finally being broken. The surviving conspirators would face justice, the victims' families would receive compensation, and new safety regulations would be implemented to prevent similar tragedies.

Patricia Henley arrived at the clinic that afternoon, her face showing the strain of the past few months but also a new sense of hope. She'd no doubt heard about Charles Ashford's death and understood that her long quest for justice was finally approaching its conclusion.

"Mr Collins, is it true? Is Charles Ashford really dead?"

"He's dead. And before he died, he confessed to arranging the murder of your brother and the four other miners. His confession was recorded, and it will be used to prosecute everyone else involved in the conspiracy."

Patricia sat down heavily in one of the clinic's chairs, the weight of months of fear and anger finally beginning to lift from her shoulders. "I still can't believe it's over. I've been living with this for so long, carrying the knowledge of what happened to Michael, that I'd almost convinced myself that justice was impossible."

"Justice was delayed, but it wasn't denied. Your courage in gathering evidence about the conspiracy made it possible to expose the truth. Without your investigation, without the risks you took, Charles Ashford might never have been held accountable for his crimes."

"What happens now?"

"Now you'll need to prepare for the trials of the surviving conspirators. The mine supervisors who carried out the sabotage, the safety inspectors who were bribed to ignore the dangerous conditions, the government officials who covered up the investigation—all of them will face justice."

"And me? What charges will I face?"

"Probably fraud for the forged credentials and extortion for the blackmail note. But given the circumstances, given that you were seeking justice for your brother's murder, I suspect you'll receive a suspended sentence. Especially if you testify against the surviving conspirators."

Patricia nodded, understanding that her actions had placed her in legal jeopardy but also knowing that she would do the same thing again if necessary. "Michael and the others deserved justice. If I have to face prison to make sure they get it, then that's a price I'm willing to pay."

"I don't think it will come to that. The public will understand why you did what you did, and the prosecutors will take that into account when they decide what charges to file."

The following weeks were a blur of statements, interviews, and legal preparations. Tom Majors coordinated with prosecutors in Sydney and Wollongong to build cases against the surviving conspirators. Dr Whitman provided detailed testimony and documentation about the coercion she'd faced and the techniques she'd used to manipulate Robert's memories. Patricia supplied the information and evidence she'd gathered about the mining conspiracy.

The first arrests came three weeks after Charles Ashford's death, when police took Bill Crawford and two other mine supervisors into custody for their role in sabotaging the tunnel supports. The men had been paid substantial bonuses for their participation in the murder scheme, and they faced charges of conspiracy to commit murder and criminal negligence.

The safety inspector who had filed the fraudulent report about the tunnel collapse was arrested at his comfortable home in Manly, where he'd been living on the proceeds of Charles Ashford's bribes. His files contained evidence of other cover-ups, other accidents that had been deliberately caused to eliminate troublesome workers.

Government officials who had suppressed the investigation were quietly forced to resign, their careers destroyed by the scandal. The Minister for Mines faced calls for his resignation after it was revealed that he'd been aware of safety problems at the Ashford operations but had failed to take action.

The trials began six months after Charles Ashford's death, with Patricia Henley serving as the key witness in the prosecution of the mining conspiracy. Her testimony was powerful and emotional, describing her brother's final letter about the dangerous conditions and his fear that workers who complained about safety violations would be targeted for elimination.

Dr Whitman's testimony revealed the psychological manipulation that had been used to prevent Robert from exposing the truth about the murders. Her description of the coercion she'd faced and the techniques she'd been forced to use painted a picture of a conspiracy that had reached into every aspect of the cover-up.

The recordings of Charles Ashford's confession provided the final piece of evidence needed to convict the surviving conspirators. No high-priced solicitor could make anything positive out of it. Ashford's casual admission that he'd arranged for the miners to die, his explanation of how he'd coerced Dr Whitman into manipulating his son's memories, his justification for treating murder as a business decision—all of it was captured on tape, providing irrefutable proof of the conspiracy.

The verdicts came after further weeks of testimony from victims' families, mining experts, and government officials. Bill Crawford and his fellow supervisors were convicted of conspiracy to commit murder and sentenced to life in prison. The safety inspector received twenty years for his role in the cover-up. Lesser figures in the conspiracy faced shorter sentences, but all were held accountable for their participation in the scheme.

Patricia Henley did indeed receive a suspended sentence for her role in exposing the conspiracy, with the judge noting that her actions had been motivated by a desire for justice rather than personal gain. Dr Whitman faced disciplinary action from the medical board but was allowed to continue practicing after demonstrating that she'd been coerced into participating in the conspiracy. Whether any patients would be willing to trust her with their ailments in the future was an open mystery that only time could solve.

The compensation payments to the victims' families were substantial, funded by the seizure of Charles Ashford's assets and the mining company's insurance policies. The families of the murdered miners received enough money to ensure their financial security, while new safety regulations were implemented throughout the NSW coal mining industry.

As I later reflected on the case in my Castlereagh Street office, I thought about the chain of events that had led to Charles Ashford's death on the mountain precipice. The mining accident had been the first link in a seam of crime that had stretched from the coalface to the psychiatric clinic to the deadly confrontation in the Blue Mountains.

But the seam had finally been broken. The truth about the mining murders had been exposed, the surviving conspirators had been prosecuted, and the victims' families had received the justice they deserved. The black seam of corruption that had run through Charles Ashford's empire had been sealed, and new safeguards had been put in place to prevent similar tragedies.

The cost had been high—six men dead, careers destroyed, families shattered, reputations ruined. But the principle had been upheld that power couldn't triumph over truth, that justice was possible even when the official system had failed, that ordinary people like Patricia Henley could make a difference by refusing to accept that corruption was inevitable. For one brief moment, the little guy had won.

The black seam had been dangerous because it was unstable and because it was controlled by men who valued profit over human life. The seam of corruption that Charles Ashford had created had been equally dangerous, running through every level of society and poisoning everything it touched.

But both seams had finally been sealed. The dangerous coal vein where the miners had died had been permanently closed, and the network of corruption that had protected their killers had been exposed and dismantled. The light of justice had finally penetrated the darkness that had hidden these crimes for so long.

The chain of corruption that had started with industrial murder had finally been broken, but the chain of justice that had replaced it would continue to grow stronger. The trials and convictions had been an ending, but they had also been a beginning—the start of a new era where worker safety would be protected, where corporate greed would be held accountable, where the truth would finally triumph over power.

The black seam was sealed, but the light of justice would continue to shine, ensuring that the sacrifice of Michael Henley and the four other miners would never be forgotten, and that their deaths would serve as a permanent reminder of the price of corruption and the value of truth.

~ Chapter 10 ~

The morning rain drummed against the windows of my Castlereagh Street office as I sat reviewing the final reports from the trials that had concluded just two weeks earlier. The newspapers had moved on to other stories, but the consequences of the Ashford conspiracy continued to ripple through the corridors of power in Sydney and throughout the coal mining communities of New South Wales.

Dr Eleanor Whitman knocked on my door at precisely ten o'clock, her posture straighter than I'd seen it in months. The woman who had first approached me about the blackmail note seemed transformed—still bearing the weight of what she'd been forced to do, but no longer crushed by the fear that had dominated her life during Charles Ashford's reign of terror.

"Mr Collins, I wanted to thank you again for everything you've done. The medical board has officially closed their investigation, and I've been cleared to continue practicing without restrictions."

"You were lucky, Dr Whitman. Your testimony was crucial to convicting the surviving conspirators, and your cooperation helped expose the full scope of the conspiracy. They obviously took all that into account. You may have a hard time rebuilding your practice, but I wish you well all the same."

She settled into the chair across from my desk, her hands folded carefully in her lap. "I keep thinking about Robert Ashford, about what I did to him under his father's coercion. The techniques I used to suppress his memories, the way I manipulated his mind to prevent him from exposing the truth about those murdered miners."

"You were operating under duress, threatened with professional and personal destruction if you didn't cooperate. The recordings of Charles Ashford's confession made that clear to everyone involved in the legal proceedings."

"But Robert is still dead. And those five miners are still dead. My actions, even under coercion, contributed to a seam of events that cost six men their lives. I will forever have all that upon my conscience."

I understood her guilt, her need to find some way to make amends for her role in the conspiracy. The medical board had exonerated her, the courts had recognized her as a victim rather than a perpetrator, but she would carry the weight of those deaths for the rest of her life. Perhaps that was, despite her final good deeds, the sort of justice that she herself deserved.

"What will you do now? Continue your practice, I assume?"

"I'm planning to establish a foundation for ethical medical research, specifically focused on preventing the kind of coercive treatments that I was forced to use on Robert." Her voice grew stronger as she spoke. "I want to ensure that no other psychiatrist is ever placed in the position I was in, that no other patient suffers the way Robert did."

"That sounds like a worthy use of your experience."

"I've also been in contact with Patricia Henley about her plans for the mining safety foundation. We're exploring ways to collaborate, to create a comprehensive approach to preventing the kind of corruption that led to her brother's death."

The mention of Patricia brought a smile to my face. The woman who had infiltrated Dr Whitman's clinic under false credentials had become a powerful advocate for industrial safety, using her brother's compensation money to fund investigations into mining accidents throughout the state. Despite her somewhat questionable initial methods in her quest for justice, I liked her.

"How is Patricia adjusting to her new role?"

"She's remarkable, Mr Collins. Her suspended sentence has allowed her to channel her anger into constructive action, and she's been working with union leaders and safety inspectors to implement the new regulations that were mandated after the trials."

"The regulations that should have been in place before her brother and the others died."

"Yes, but at least they're in place now. And Patricia has made it clear that she'll be watching to ensure they're actually enforced, not just written into law and then ignored."

When Dr Whitman finally left, her step was lighter than when she'd arrived. The woman had found a way to transform her guilt into action, to use her professional skills to prevent other tragedies like the one that had destroyed so many lives.

But the real test of whether justice had been served would come later that afternoon, when I traveled to Wollongong for the memorial service that Patricia had organised for her brother and the four other miners who had died in Charles Ashford's engineered collapse.

I decided to drive rather than take the train as I had during my earlier investigations. The long journey would give me time to think about the case and what it had revealed about the nature of justice and corruption in New South Wales. The familiar rhythm of the train had suited the investigative phase of the case, but now I wanted the solitude and control that came with driving my own automobile.

The drive south through the industrial landscape of the Illawarra took me past the coal mines and steel mills that formed the economic backbone of the region. But I also noticed the new safety equipment that had been installed at the mining operations, the warning signs that had been posted at dangerous work sites, the evidence that the deaths of five men had finally led to meaningful change.

The memorial service was held at the same small church in Wollongong where the miners' families had gathered for the original funerals almost two years earlier. But this time, the atmosphere was different—still sorrowful, but also defiant, determined to ensure that the men's deaths would serve as a permanent reminder of the price of industrial corruption.

Patricia Henley stood at the podium, her voice carrying clearly through the packed church as she addressed the assembled crowd of miners, union officials, and family members. She wore a simple black dress, but her bearing was that of a woman who had transformed her grief into a weapon for justice.

"Michael and the others knew they were in danger when they decided to report the unsafe conditions in the black seam," she began. "They knew that speaking out about the negligence could cost them their jobs, maybe even their lives. But they also knew that someone had to stand up for the workers who couldn't protect themselves."

The congregation listened in absolute silence as Patricia described her brother's final letter, his fear that workers who complained about safety violations would be targeted for elimination, his determination to expose the truth despite the personal risk.

"Michael wrote to me about the dangerous conditions in the seam where he was working, about the warnings that were ignored by management, about the pressure from Charles Ashford to keep the mine operating despite the safety hazards." Her voice grew stronger. "He knew that reporting these conditions might make him a target, but he also knew that staying silent would mean that other workers would die."

Her words brought it all back to me, the blackmail letter which herladed my entry into the case and the investigation that had led from Patricia's infiltration of Dr Whitman's clinic to the deadly confrontation in the Blue Mountains where Charles Ashford had fallen to his death. The black seam that had killed her brother had ultimately claimed the life of the man who had engineered the collapse.

"The men who died in that tunnel weren't just statistics in a mining accident report," Patricia continued. "They were fathers and brothers, husbands and sons. They were men who worked dangerous jobs to support their families, who trusted their employers to provide safe working conditions, who believed that their lives mattered."

She paused, looking out over the congregation with eyes that held both sorrow and steel. "Charles Ashford and his associates treated these men as disposable, as obstacles to be eliminated when they threatened to expose the truth about the unsafe conditions. But their deaths weren't meaningless—they've led to changes that will protect other workers, that will prevent similar tragedies."

The service continued with testimonials from the families of the other murdered miners, each one describing a man who had been more than just a victim of industrial greed. There was William Foster, whose wife described his dedication to his three young children and his dream of saving enough money to buy a small farm. And there was James Mooney, whose brother spoke about his love of rugby and his plans to marry his sweetheart after the next pay raise.

Tom Majors spoke about the investigation that had exposed the conspiracy, praising Patricia's courage in gathering evidence and Dr Whitman's willingness to testify despite the personal cost. He also announced that the NSW government was implementing new safety regulations throughout the coal mining industry, with penalties severe enough to deter future negligence.

"The men who died in the black seam collapse have become symbols of the need for industrial safety reform," Tom said. "Their deaths have led to changes that will save other lives, that will prevent other families from experiencing this kind of tragedy."

Others spoke, not nearly as well, and the service continued on in much the same way as it had. Finally, with the issuing of prayers, it was all said and done.

After the service, I walked through the cemetery where the five miners were buried, their graves marked with simple headstones that bore only their names and dates. But Patricia had arranged for a larger memorial to be erected, a granite monument that listed the names of all five men and included the inscription: "They died seeking truth and justice for their fellow workers."

"It's not enough," Patricia said as we stood before the memorial. "Nothing can bring them back, nothing can undo the suffering that Charles Ashford caused. But at least their deaths have meaning now, at least they've led to changes that will protect other workers."

"You've given their deaths meaning, Patricia. You've transformed tragedy into action, grief into justice."

"I've tried. But the real test will be whether the changes we've achieved are permanent, whether the safety regulations are actually enforced, whether other workers remember the price that Michael and the others paid."

The memorial service had drawn representatives from mining unions throughout New South Wales, and they had committed to establishing annual observances to honor the victims of industrial accidents. The names of Michael Henley and the four other miners would be remembered, their deaths serving as a permanent reminder of the need for workplace safety.

But Patricia had achieved something more significant than symbolic commemoration. The foundation she had established was already working with mining unions and safety inspectors to ensure that the new regulations were properly implemented and enforced. The tools and techniques she had developed during her investigation were being used to monitor compliance and investigate potential violations.

"What's next for you? Dr Whitman said you'd be collaborating with her," I asked as we walked back toward the church.

"Yes indeed. The foundation work will keep me busy. Making sure the new safety regulations are actually enforced, working with the unions to identify potential problems before they become tragedies." Her voice carried the same determination that had driven her to infiltrate the psychiatric clinic. "Michael and the others can't speak for themselves anymore, but I can speak for them. I can make sure their deaths serve as a warning to companies that think they can sacrifice worker safety for profit."

As I started my slow trudge back to my parked car, Tom came up behind me. "Moving service, Magpie." I nodded as he walked alongside me. "Thought you'd want to know. The Minister for Mines will tomorrow announce that the new safety regulations will be extended to all mining operations throughout New South Wales. They're calling it the Henley Safety Act, after Patricia's brother."

"Appropriate. Michael Henley and the others died trying to expose the very conditions that the new regulations are designed to prevent. What about the mine inspectors? Will they actually enforcing the regulations?"

"The mine owners know that the government is serious about enforcement this time, especially after what happened to Charles Ashford and his associates."

"Fear of prosecution can be a powerful motivator for corporate responsibility."

Tom raised his hand in a mock toast. "To the power of consequences. Amazing how quickly businessmen develop a conscience when they face the prospect of prison sentences."

We said our goodbyes and I got in the car and headed off through the streets of Wollongong. As I made my way back to Sydney through the twilight, I found myself thinking about the price of truth that Patricia had mentioned. Michael Henley and the four other miners had paid the ultimate price for their willingness to expose unsafe working conditions. Robert Ashford had paid with his life for discovering his father's role in the murders. Charles Ashford had paid with his fall from the mountain precipice, his empire of corruption crumbling around him.

But there had been other prices as well. Dr Whitman would carry the guilt of her coerced participation in the conspiracy for the rest of her life and perhaps her practice would never recover. Patricia would never escape the grief of losing her brother, even as she channeled that grief into a force for justice. The families of the murdered miners would always mourn their lost loved ones, even as they found some comfort in the knowledge that their deaths had led to meaningful change.

The black seam that had killed the miners had been permanently sealed, but the metaphorical seam of corruption that had connected industrial murder to psychological manipulation had been more difficult to close. The trials and convictions had exposed the conspiracy, but they had also revealed how easily truth could be suppressed, how readily officials could be bought, how completely the powerful could dominate the powerless.

Yet the memorial service had also demonstrated the resilience of truth, its ability to survive even the most determined efforts to destroy it. Michael Henley's letter to his sister had preserved the evidence of the unsafe conditions. Robert Ashford's diary had documented his father's role in the murders. Patricia's investigation had gathered the proof needed to expose the conspiracy.

The truth had been buried like a coal seam, hidden beneath layers of lies and corruption and official indifference. But it had also been durable like coal, capable of burning brightly when finally exposed to the light of justice. The memorial service had been a celebration of that durability, a recognition that truth might be suppressed but could never be completely destroyed.

The price of truth had been high—six men dead, careers destroyed, families shattered. But the alternative price, the cost of allowing corruption to continue unchecked, would have been even higher. How many more workers would have died in unsafe conditions? How many more families would have been destroyed by industrial negligence? How many more Robert Ashfords would have been driven to suicide by the weight of suppressed knowledge?

As I reached the outskirts of Sydney, I could see the lights of the city spreading out before me, the industrial landscape giving way to the commercial and residential districts that formed the heart of New South Wales. The case had taken me from the psychiatric clinics of Woollahra to the coal mines of the Illawarra, from the Blue Mountains estates of the wealthy to the boarding houses of Katoomba where the desperate tried to escape their past.

But the drive tonight felt different from those earlier journeys. Then I had been pursuing leads, following clues, trying to understand the connections between blackmail and murder, between industrial accidents and psychiatric manipulation. Now I was returning from a memorial service that had provided a sense of closure, not just for the families of the victims but for everyone who had been touched by the conspiracy.

The black seam of overall corruption would never be completely sealed. There would always be other Charles Ashfords, other men willing to sacrifice lives for their own interests. But there would also be other Patricia Henleys, other people willing to fight for truth and justice regardless of the personal cost.

The memorial service had been both an ending and a beginning. It had provided closure for the families of the murdered miners, but it had also launched a new phase of

Patricia's campaign for industrial safety. The foundation she had established would continue the work that her brother and the others had started, ensuring that their deaths would serve as a permanent bulwark against corporate negligence.

The most important legacy of the case would be the principle that had been established: that truth could triumph over power, that justice was possible even when the official system had failed, that ordinary people could make a difference by refusing to accept that corruption was inevitable. Sometimes the little guy *could* win over the big end of town. That alone was worth it all for me.

I pulled into the parking space behind my office building, and I knew that tomorrow would bring new cases, new mysteries, new challenges. But tonight, I was content to know that *this* black seam of corruption that had claimed six lives had finally been sealed, and that the light of justice would continue to shine on the memory of those who had paid the ultimate price for truth.

~ Author's Note ~

I was most gratified with my first book in this new series, *The Broken Chain*, and by readers reaction to it, that I was instantly drawn to crafting the next chapter in the series as quickly as possible. And I was eager for 'Magpie' Collins to venture south to my hometown of Wollongong equally as quickly. Much like the master Ross MacDonald's Lew Archer books, I want my detective to travel beyond the confines of Sydney as the story dictates, and this book is just the first of such stories planned in the future. If you continue reading, you'll see an excerpt from the next in the series, *The Magpie's Shadow*, in the following pages. Please look for that to release just before Christmas 2025.

As always, there are people I'd like to thank. My family are first and foremost. My wife and daughter give my life meaning, and are the backbone of my support team. Without them I am nothing. My mother, sister and my in-law's are also very important to me. My sincerest thanks to them all.

Thanks to my team here at Glowing Eyes Media, Chaz and Claude. Your talents helped hone this story into what it has become. I value your input and look forward to working with you in the future on every 'Magpie' Collins story.

The ultimate thanks, as always, goes to you, my dear readers. Every story I craft is for your benefit as much as it is for my own. I hope you enjoyed this one and I certainly hope you are looking forward to the next one and beyond. I'm excited about the future.

All the best.

Frank Dirscherl aka Len Driscoll
Wollongong, 2025

THE MAGPIE'S SHADOW

~ Sneak peek ~

Here is a special sneak peek at the following novel in the series, *The Magpie's Shadow*. Please enjoy chapter 1 of this exciting book...

~ Chapter 1 ~

A cold winter rain drummed against the grimy windows of my second-floor office like impatient fingers tapping on a bar top. I sat behind my desk, nursing a cup of black coffee that had gone cold an hour ago, watching the water streak down the glass in irregular patterns that reminded me of the tears on a fence's face when the coppers finally caught up with him. The view from my window on Castlereagh Street wasn't much—just the wet brick wall of the building opposite and a narrow slice of grey Sydney sky that promised more rain before the day was through.

It was Thursday, the fifteenth of July, 1935, and business had been slower than a funeral procession. The sign on my door read 'George Collins, Private Investigator' in faded gold lettering that had seen better days. I used to work outside the law, as a jewel thief of some little renown. In those days, my nickname had been 'Magpie', due to my predilection for all things sparkly. Nowadays, the only one who still called me that was my good friend, Police Chief Tom Majors, the man who helped me see sense and assisted in my acquiring my investigator's licence. These days, my particular knowledge of criminal behaviour came in handy in helping the law-abiding citizens of Sydney solve their problems, though the irony wasn't lost on me that I was now paid to catch the sort of bloke I used to be.

The rain had been falling steadily for three days, turning the streets into rivers and keeping most sensible people indoors. I'd spent the morning reading the day's *Sydney Morning Herald* and trying to make sense of the political situation in Europe, where that Austrian madman with the Charlie Chaplin moustache was making increasingly unpleasant noises about his neighbours. Closer to home, the Labor Party was making headway in the state parliament, which suited me fine. I'd always believed that a fair day's work deserved a fair day's pay, and that the bloke in the expensive suit shouldn't get rich off the sweat of the working man's brow.

I was contemplating whether to venture next door to the NSW Masonic Club for a late breakfast when I heard footsteps in the corridor outside my office. They were light, measured steps—a woman's heels clicking against the worn linoleum with the kind of precision that spoke of breeding and money. The footsteps paused outside my door, and I heard the rustle of clothing as someone read the nameplate. A moment later, a soft knock echoed through the room.

"Come in," I called, straightening my tie and pushing the newspaper aside.

The door opened to reveal a woman who belonged in the society pages of the newspaper rather than in the shabby office of a reformed criminal turned private detective. She was somewhere in her forties, I estimated, with dark auburn hair styled in perfect waves and a complexion that spoke of regular visits to expensive beauty salons. Her navy blue dress was cut from expensive fabric and tailored to perfection, and she carried herself with the kind of poise that comes from never having to worry about where her next meal was coming from. Everything about her screamed money, from the pearl earrings that caught the grey light from the window to the crocodile leather handbag she clutched in gloved hands.

But it was her eyes that caught my attention. They were a striking shade of blue, the colour of sapphire, and they held a combination of desperation and determination that I'd seen before in clients who had nowhere else to turn. She stood in the doorway for a moment, taking in the spartanly furnished office with its well-used desk, two excellent though equally well-used chairs, and filing cabinet that had seen better decades.

"Mr Collins?" she asked, her voice carrying the refined accent of Sydney's eastern suburbs. "Mr George Collins?"

"That's what it says on the door," I said, standing and gesturing to the chair across from my desk. "Please, have a seat. You look like you could use a cup of coffee, though I should warn you it's not as good as what you're likely used to."

She moved into the room with fluid grace, settling into the chair and placing her handbag carefully in her lap. "Thank you, but no. I... I'm rather anxious about why I'm here."

I sat back down and leaned forward slightly, adopting what I hoped was a reassuring expression. "Most people who come to see me are anxious about something, Mrs..?"

"Hartwell," she said, then paused as if the name carried weight she wasn't sure she wanted to bear. "Mrs Evelyn Hartwell."

The name was familiar, though I couldn't immediately place it. Hartwell...it had the ring of money and influence, the sort of name that appeared in the business pages and society columns. I made a mental note to place it later, if need be, and focused on my potential client.

"Well then, Mrs Hartwell, what brings you to my office on this wet Thursday morning?"

She opened her handbag and withdrew a lace handkerchief, though her eyes were dry. It seemed to be more of a nervous gesture than a necessity. "Mr Collins, I've heard that you have a particular...expertise when it comes to matters involving jewellery."

I felt a familiar tingle at the base of my skull, the same sensation I used to get when casing a particularly promising mark. "It appears you know something of my background. I have some experience in that area, yes. What seems to be the problem?"

"My jewellery collection has been stolen," she said, her voice barely above a whisper. "Some of my most prized pieces. The police have been investigating for three days now, but they seem to have made no progress whatsoever."

"When did this happen?"

"Monday night. We were hosting a charity gala at our home in Point Piper—a fundraiser for the Children's Hospital. There were perhaps sixty guests, all quite respectable people from the best families in Sydney." She paused, dabbing at her nose with the handkerchief. "Sometime during the evening, someone entered our bedroom and opened our safe. They took my grandmother's diamond tiara, an emerald necklace that belonged to my mother, and a ruby bracelet that my husband gave me for our tenth wedding anniversary."

I pulled out a notepad and pencil, though I was already committing every detail to memory. In my former profession, a good memory could mean the difference between a successful job and a long stretch in Long Bay Gaol. "What's the estimated value of the stolen pieces?"

"Over ten thousand pounds," she said, and I tried not to whistle. That was more money than most working men saw in a lifetime, myself included. "The insurance company is being...difficult. They seem to think that because it happened during a party, we might have staged the theft ourselves."

"And did you?"

The question hung in the air between us like smoke from a cheap cigarette. Mrs Hartwell's blue eyes flashed with something that might have been anger, but it was gone so quickly I couldn't be sure.

"Mr Collins, I came to you because I was told you were discreet and effective. I was also told that you had a particular understanding of how thieves operate. I was not told that you would insult me within five minutes of our meeting."

I held up a hand in what I hoped was a placating gesture. "Mrs Hartwell, I apologise if I offended you. But in my line of work, I have to ask the questions that might be uncomfortable. Insurance fraud is more common than you might think, even among the best families. If I'm going to help you, I need to know everything, including whether there might be any reason someone would suspect you of staging the theft."

She was quiet for a long moment, staring out the rain-streaked window to her right. When she spoke again, her voice was softer, more vulnerable. "My husband's import business has been struggling lately. The Depression hit everyone hard, even those of us who thought we were immune. But Mr Collins, I swear to you on my mother's grave that neither my husband nor I had anything to do with this theft. Someone came into our home during what should have been a joyous occasion and violated our privacy, our security. I want them caught and punished."

There was something in her voice that convinced me she was telling the truth, at least about her own innocence. But there was also something she wasn't telling me, something that made her avoid my eyes when she spoke about her husband. In my experience, the things people didn't say were often more important than the things they did.

"When did you discover the theft? And when were the police called?"

"We discovered it the next morning, Tuesday, when I went to put away some jewellery I'd worn to the party. The safe door was closed, but when I opened it..." She shuddered slightly. "The three most valuable pieces were gone. My husband called the police immediately."

"And what did the police tell you about how the safe was opened?"

"That's what's so strange," she said, leaning forward in her chair. "The detective—Inspector Morrison, I think his name was—said there were no signs of forced entry. No scratches on the lock, no damage to the door. Whoever opened it knew the combination."

"Who else knew the combination besides you and your husband?"

"No one. At least, no one was supposed to know. We never wrote it down, never told anyone." She paused, biting her lower lip. "Although..."

"Although what?"

"Well, the safe is quite old. My husband's father installed it when he built the house thirty years ago. I suppose it's possible that someone who worked on the house might have learned the combination somehow."

I made another note. "What about your household staff? How long have they worked for you?"

"Our butler, Arthur Pemberton, has been with the family for fifteen years. He's absolutely trustworthy. Rose Murphy, our housemaid, has been with us for three years. She's a good girl, very reliable. And our cook, Mrs Patterson, has been with us for nearly eight years."

"Any recent changes in staff? Anyone new who might have had access to the house?"

Mrs Hartwell shook her head. "No, our staff has been quite stable. We treat them well and pay them fairly."

I leaned back in my chair, studying her face. She was beautiful, there was no denying that, but there was something brittle about her beauty, like fine porcelain that might crack under pressure. And there was definitely pressure here, though I wasn't sure yet what kind.

"Mrs Hartwell, I have to ask—is there anyone who might have a grudge against you or your husband? Any business rivals, former employees who were dismissed, anyone who might want to hurt you?"

For the first time since she'd entered my office, Mrs Hartwell looked genuinely uncomfortable. She shifted in her chair and her grip tightened on her handbag. "My husband's business dealings are quite complex, Mr Collins. He imports tea and silk from China, and there's always competition in that trade. But I can't think of anyone who would resort to theft."

"What about personal enemies? Social rivals?"

"We move in the best circles of Sydney society, Mr Collins. One doesn't make enemies in such circles, at least not openly." But even as she said it, I could see in her eyes that she was thinking of someone specific.

"Mrs Hartwell, if I'm going to help you, I need complete honesty. Is there someone you're thinking of?"

She was quiet for so long I thought she might not answer. Finally, she sighed and said, "There's the Weatherby family. Judge Harold Weatherby and his son Charles. There was...an unpleasant business matter between my husband and the Judge some years ago. Nothing criminal, you understand, just a dispute over import licences and trading rights. It left some bad feelings."

"Bad enough for someone to break into your house and steal your jewellery?"

"I...I don't know. I wouldn't have thought so, but..." She trailed off, staring at her hands.

"But what?"

"Charles Weatherby was at the party on Monday night. I saw him talking to several of our guests, and he seemed to know his way around the house quite well. Perhaps too well."

I made a note of the name Weatherby. In my criminal days, I'd learned that family feuds could motivate people to do things they'd never normally consider. And I'd heard of the Judge. If Charles Weatherby was familiar with the Hartwell house, he might have had opportunities to learn about the safe.

"Mrs Hartwell, what exactly do you want me to do? The police are already investigating. Why come to a private detective?"

She looked directly at me for the first time since she'd mentioned the Weatherbys, and I saw something desperate in her sapphire blue eyes. "Because the police seem more interested in proving that we staged the theft than in finding the real thief. Because I need someone who understands how criminals think and operate. And because..." She paused, then continued in a rush, "Because I'm afraid this is about more than just jewellery."

"What do you mean?"

"I think someone is trying to destroy my husband's reputation, to ruin him financially and socially. The theft happened during a charity event, Mr Collins. Half of Sydney's social elite were in our home that night. By now, everyone knows that our private safe was robbed while we were entertaining guests. People are already starting to whisper that we must have staged it for the insurance money."

I could see her point. In Sydney's tight-knit high society, reputation was everything. A suggestion of financial impropriety could destroy a man's business and social standing faster than a house fire.

"What's your husband's position on hiring me?"

"He...he doesn't know I'm here." She looked down at her hands again. "Edgar thinks we should trust the police to handle the matter. He says hiring a private detective would only make us look more guilty."

"But you disagreed."

"I can't just sit and wait while our reputation is destroyed and our belongings remain in the hands of thieves. I need to do something."

I studied her face for a moment, trying to read the emotions playing across her features. There was determination there, and desperation, but also something else —fear. She was afraid of something, and I didn't think it was just the loss of her jewellery.

"My fee is five pounds a day plus expenses," I said finally. "I'll need a retainer of twenty-five pounds to start."

Relief flooded her face. "Of course. Whatever you require." She opened her handbag and withdrew a roll of banknotes that would have been impressive even in my thieving days. She counted out twenty-five pounds and placed them on my desk.

"I'll also need a detailed description of the stolen pieces, a list of everyone who attended the party, and access to your house so I can examine the scene."

"Certainly. I have photographs of the jewellery at home, and I can provide you with the guest list." She paused. "When can you start?"

"I've already started, Mrs Hartwell. But I should warn you —if I uncover something you don't want to know, something that might be embarrassing to you or your husband, I won't stop investigating just because it makes you uncomfortable."

"I understand. I just want the truth, Mr Collins. Whatever it might be."

As she said it, I had the distinct impression that Mrs Evelyn Hartwell was lying, at least to herself. In my experience, people who said they wanted the truth usually wanted a version of the truth that didn't hurt too much. But that was her problem. My job was to find out what really happened to her jewellery, and if that led to uncomfortable revelations, so be it.

"I'll need your address and telephone number," I said, pulling out a client information form.

"We live at Bellevue Hill, Point Piper. The house is called 'Tara'—it's on the harbour with a circular drive. You can't miss it." She gave me the telephone number and I wrote it down carefully.

"One more question, Mrs Hartwell. These pieces that were stolen—were they just valuable, or did they have sentimental value as well?"

"Both," she said, and for the first time I heard genuine emotion in her voice. "The tiara belonged to my grandmother. She wore it at her wedding in 1851. The emerald necklace was my mother's favourite piece—she wore it to every important social event for twenty years. And the ruby bracelet..." She paused, touching her wrist unconsciously. "My husband gave it to me on our tenth wedding anniversary. He said the rubies matched the fire in my hair."

"So whoever took them didn't just steal valuable jewellery. They stole pieces of your family history."

"Exactly." She stood up, smoothing down her dress. "That's why I need them back, Mr Collins. The money isn't the important thing. Even our reputation isn't everything. It's what those pieces represent."

I stood as well, coming around the desk to walk her to the door. "I'll start by examining your house this afternoon, if that's convenient. I'd like to see the safe and talk to your staff."

"Of course. I'll make sure they're available to speak with you." She paused at the door, turning back to face me. "Mr Collins, may I ask you something personal?"

"You can ask. Can't guarantee I'll answer."

"Why did you give up your previous...profession...to become a private detective?"

It was a fair question, one I used to ask myself often enough. "Let's just say I discovered that there's more satisfaction in catching thieves than in being one."

She smiled for the first time since entering my office, and it transformed her face completely. "I hope you're as good at catching them as I hear you were at being one."

"So do I, Mrs Hartwell. So do I."

After she left, I sat back down at my desk and stared at the twenty-five pounds she'd given me. It was more money than I'd seen in months, and it represented the difference between paying my rent and being evicted. But more than that, it represented a case that might actually be interesting. Jewellery thefts, by their and my former nature, were a speciality of mine, of a sort, and this one had all the elements of a proper puzzle—a locked safe opened without force, valuable items stolen during a social gathering, and a client who was clearly not telling me everything she knew.

I picked up the telephone and dialed the number for police headquarters. When the desk sergeant answered, I asked to speak to Tom Majors.

"Magpie!" Tom's voice boomed through the earpiece. "Haven't heard from you in a little while. How's business?"

"Can't complain, Tom. Listen, I've just been hired to look into a jewellery theft in Point Piper. Hartwell is the name. What can you tell me about it?"

There was a pause, then Tom's voice came back in a more serious tone. "Edgar Hartwell, the importer? Yeah, we've got a file on that one. Happened Monday night during some charity do. Professional job, by the look of it. Safe was opened clean, no damage to the door or lock mechanism."

"Any suspects?"

"Nothing concrete. Could have been an inside job—someone who knew the combination and the layout of the house. Or it could have been a professional who got the combination somehow. We're still working on it."

"Mind if I take a look at the scene?"

"Would you stop if I said no?" He said with a chuckle, then sighed. "By all means. See if you can unearth something we missed. If you do, you'll let me know, right?"

"Always do. Thanks, Tom."

I hung up the phone and leaned back in my chair, thinking about what I'd learned so far. Mrs Hartwell appeared to be hiding something, that much was clear to me. Her husband didn't know she'd hired me, which suggested either that he was opposed to the idea or that she didn't trust him completely. The theft had been professional, which meant either an experienced criminal or someone with inside knowledge. And there was this business with the Weatherby family, which might be nothing or might be the key to everything.

I looked out the window at the rain, which showed no signs of letting up, and confirmed my earlier decision. I'd take the tram out to Point Piper this afternoon and have a look at the scene of the crime. The Hartwell house and its compromised safe might tell me more than Mrs Hartwell's carefully edited version of events.

But first, I checked my Longines Evidenza wrist watch. Time for an early lunch. I locked the money in my desk drawer, put on my coat and hat, and headed next door to the NSW Masonic Club. The dining room was warm and dry, filled with the comfortable smell of roast beef and tobacco smoke. I found a table by the window where I could watch the rain and think about the case while I ate.

As I waited for my meal, I thought about Mrs Evelyn Hartwell and her stolen jewellery. There was something about the case that reminded me of the old days, when I'd study a mark for weeks before making my move. The careful observation, the patient gathering of information, the gradual understanding of how all the pieces fit together. The only difference was that now I was on the other side of the law, using those same skills to catch thieves instead of being one.

The irony wasn't lost on me that my criminal past made me uniquely qualified to understand how this particular crime might have been committed. I knew how professional thieves operated, what they looked for in a target, how they gathered information and planned their moves. If the Hartwell robbery was the work of a professional, I had a better chance than most of figuring out how it was done and who did it.

But if it was an inside job, as Tom suspected, then it became a different sort of puzzle entirely. Inside jobs were messier, more personal. They involved betrayal and secrets, family dynamics and hidden resentments. They were harder to solve because the motives were often more complex than simple greed.

As I ate my steak and sipped my beer, I found myself thinking about shadows. There were shadows everywhere in this case: the shadow of Mrs Hartwell's fear, the shadow of her husband's possible financial troubles, the shadow of the Weatherby family feud, and perhaps most relevantly, the shadow of my own criminal past that qualified me to investigate the crime.

In my thieving days, I'd learned that shadows could hide important things, but they could also reveal them if you knew how to look. The angle of a shadow could tell you the time of day, the position of obstacles, the best route of escape. In detective work, I had already realised, shadows worked much the same way. The things people didn't say, the glances they avoided, the topics they changed too quickly—these shadows might be more revealing than the facts they were trying to hide.

By the time I finished my meal, the rain had lightened to a steady drizzle. I paid my bill and headed back to my office next door to collect my notebook and camera. It was time to visit the scene of the crime and see what the shadows at the Hartwell house might reveal.

As I locked up my office and headed for the tram stop, I couldn't shake the feeling that this case was going to be more complicated than a simple jewellery theft. Mrs Hartwell's nervousness, her husband's opposition to hiring a private detective, the professional nature of the job, and the timing during a social gathering all suggested layers of complexity that I was only beginning to understand.

But that was what made detective work interesting. Like my old profession, it required patience, observation, and the ability to see patterns that others missed. The only difference was that now I was using those skills in service of justice rather than personal gain.

The tram was nearly empty as it carried me through the wet streets toward Point Piper and whatever secrets the Hartwell house might be hiding. I stared out the rain-streaked windows and wondered what I would find, and whether the Hartwell family would be pleased with whatever secrets I might uncover.

~ Also Available ~

A George 'Magpie' Collins Mystery #1

THE BROKEN CHAIN

Len Driscoll

In depression-era Sydney, young Charlie Bristow has vanished without a trace. Enter George 'Magpie' Collins, ex-con turned private investigator, hired to find the troubled youth As he delves into the shadows of the city, Collins must navigate the murky waters of deception and bring justice to a broken chain.

NOW AVAILABLE!

www.glowingeyesmedia.com

VALLEY OF EVIL

The Wraith Dread Avenger of the Underworld #2
VALLEY OF EVIL
Frank Dirscherl

After the horror the Cobra unleashed upon Metro City, Paul
Sanderson has recuperated, regained his strength and focus, and
the city has been rebuilt while its citizens have slowly started to
regroup and move forward. Into this relative calm marches Ma Tzi,
the Hong Kong drug lord, who senses a weakness in resident crime
lord Robert Latham's hold on the city and intends to exploit that
in any way necessary. And at any cost.

NOW AVAILABLE!

www.glowingeyesmedia.com

The Wraith Dread Avenger of the Underworld #3
CROSSFIRE
Stephen J. Semones & Frank Dirscherl

After a terrorist attack leaves the citizens of Metro City reeling, an enigmatic stranger emerges from the wake of the destruction to wage war on local crime-lord Robert Latham. In the midst of this, Max Horton, The Wraith's right-hand man, vanishes without a trace. Searching for Max, and for those responsible for the devastation, The Wraith sets out for answers.

NOW AVAILABLE!

www.glowingeyesmedia.com

The Wraith Dread Avenger of the Underworld #4
CULT OF THE DAMNED
Frank Dirscherl

With the city back firmly in his grasp, crime lord and entrepreneur Robert Latham is celebrating by bankrolling Metro City's 200th anniversary gala year, which includes the unveiling of a never-before-seen ancient Aztec stone carving—the Cortes Stone—at the City Gallery, a carving that has thrilled the scientific and artistic communities, but infuriated the monstrous Aztekoth.

NOW AVAILABLE!

www.glowingeyesmedia.com

The Wraith Dread Avenger of the Underworld #5
CRY OF THE WEREWOLF
Frank Dirscherl

Having gone through ordeal after ordeal, Paul Sanderson (aka The Wraith Dread Avenger of the Underworld ®) and his love Leena Patterson, decide to take a long overdue vacation. However, their idyll is soon shattered by an attack by a creature nobody thought could possibly exist—a werewolf. Soon, an evil so heinous makes himself known, and only The Wraith could possibly defeat it.

NOW AVAILABLE!

www.glowingeyesmedia.com

The Wraith Dread Avenger of the Underworld #6
SWAMP WITCH OF SATAN'S FOREST
Frank Dirscherl & Ray MacKay

On their way home from their mountain vacation which was
anything but, Paul Sanderson (aka The Wraith) and his love Leena
Patterson are waylaid by a mysterious cry for help, and are
unwittingly drawn into the forest—and the web—of the alluring
Swamp Witch.

NOW AVAILABLE!

www.glowingeyesmedia.com

The Wraith Dread Avenger of the Underworld #7
VENDETTA
Frank Dirscherl

After having been betrayed by crime lord, Robert Latham, and defeated by The Wraith, Crossfire has returned to cause mayhem and carnage at every turn. His ultimate aim? The utter destruction of all his enemies, and he doesn't care who gets in his way.

NOW AVAILABLE!

www.glowingeyesmedia.com

The Wraith Dread Avenger of the Underworld #8
LADY WRAITH
Frank Dirscherl & Adam Oravec

The Wraith is missing. No one has seen him since going out on patrol. Now, the love of his life Leena Patterson, must sally forth on her own as Lady Wraith, protect the city, find her love, and combat a deadly new adversary hell-bent on destruction.

NOW AVAILABLE!

www.glowingeyesmedia.com

The Wraith Dread Avenger of the Underworld #9
KINGDOM
Frank Dirscherl

Crime lord, Robert Latham has returned, seemingly from the dead, ready to reclaim his kingdom. Ready to take whatever steps are necessary to restock and rebuild, to recover his rightful position within Metro City, and he doesn't care who gets in his way.

NOW AVAILABLE!

www.glowingeyesmedia.com

The Wraith Dread Avenger of the Underworld
#11
BIRDS OF THE LIVING DEAD
Frank Dirscherl

The dead are being re-animated, marching through Metro City, causing carnage throughout. Can The Wraith figure out what is going on, fight this undead menace, and find whomever is responsible? And what of the giant vultures plaguing the city? All this and more in this masterful tale of suspense and adventure.

COMING SOON!

www.glowingeyesmedia.com

Books of Judgment Book One
SANDERSON OF METRO
Frank Dirscherl & Bobby Nash

Two masters of the pulp fiction world, Frank Dirscherl and Bobby Nash, have come together to tell this tale, the secret NEVER before told origin of the first Wraith/Paul Sanderson, as only they could. This action-packed, atmospheric thrill could only be told now, and it could only be told by master storytellers like Dirscherl and Nash. An epic never to be repeated and not to be missed.

NOW AVAILABLE!

www.glowingeyesmedia.com

Books of Judgment Book Two
SERPENT RISING
Frank Dirscherl & Greg Gick

The never-before-told origin story of The Wraith's arch nemesis the
Cobra. Who he is, how he came to be, and how his and the
original Paul Sanderson's life intertwined at key moments to cause
them to become deadly adversaries. It's all here!

NOW AVAILABLE!

www.glowingeyesmedia.com

Books of Judgment Book Three
RISING SON
Frank Dirscherl & Adam Oravec

Robert Latham, Metro City's pre-eminent businessman and entrepreneur. He's also the head of the largest crime cartel on the east coast, the web in the center of the city's web of evil. But how did he become the all-powerful figure within the city. Growing up with nothing, he built his empire from the ground up, through strength, determination, and cold-blooded intimidation.

COMING SOON!

www.glowingeyesmedia.com

About the Type

Garamond is a group of many old-style serif typefaces, originally those designed by Parisian craftsman Claude Garamond and other 16th century French engravers, and now many modern revivals. Though his name was written as 'Garamont' in his lifetime, the typefaces are generally spelled 'Garamond'. **Garamond Normal**, used in this book, is one of those modern revivals.

Join FRANK DIRSCHERL and LEN DRISCOLL with Glowing Eyes Media on social media!

facebook.com/glowingeyesmedia

@glowingeyesmedia

instagram.com/glowingeyesmedia

@glowingeyesmedia.bsky.social

glowingeyesmedia.proboards.com

All Glowing Eyes Media, The Wraith, George 'Magpie' Collins novels, comics and merchandise can be obtained directly from the Glowing Eyes Media website – www.glowingeyesmedia.com

www.ingramcontent.com/pod-product-compliance
Lightning Source LLC
Chambersburg PA
CBHW051126260626
47170CB00005B/1692